Under Orion

Books by Janice Law

The Big Payoff
Gemini Trip
Under Orion

Under Orion

Janice Law

Houghton Mifflin Company
Boston 1978

HOUSTON PUBLIC LIBRARY

Library of Congress Cataloging in Publication Data

Law, Janice.
    Under Orion.

    I. Title
PZ4.L415Un   [PS3562.A86] 813'.5'4   78-6685
ISBN 0-395-26484-7

Printed in the United States of America
s 10 9 8 7 6 5 4 3 2 1

For Audrey and Harleigh Trecker

Under Orion

Chapter 1

"GOOD AFTERNOON, MR. GILSON; good afternoon, Miss Peters."

"Everything under control today, Walter?"

"Yes, thank you, sir. Will this table be suitable?"

"Fine. Is McKenzie here?"

"Not yet, sir."

"Bring him over as soon as he comes in, and get me a bourbon. What would you like, Anna?"

"Nothing for me today."

"Miss Peters doesn't trust me, Walter. Do I look as though I've reached the dangerous age?"

Walter laughed politely. In length of service, he outranked even Gilson. He knew everyone and everything, and, better yet, he knew how to keep his mouth shut. "Perhaps Miss Peters would like some juice?"

"Yes, please."

Walter headed for the bar, his dignified gray presence sending the lesser inhabitants of the executive dining room into flurries of activity. Gilson watched him with approval, then swung his heavy head to examine the rest of the diners. A phalanx of junior executives diminished under his gaze, a member of the board waved, a visiting stockbroker whispered to his companion. Gilson surveyed his domain, twisted his neck as if his immaculate collar was too tight, and consulted the menu with studied disdain. New World Oil's best cuisine suited him very well, but, like his major domo, he was ever prepared for human frailty and culinary lapses.

"I think I'll have the sole," he remarked. "Martha thinks I'm too fat."

"I'll have the same."

"We'll have the turban of sole, Walter," Gilson said when the drinks arrived.

"Very good, sir. And for Mr. McKenzie?"

"Have them call the lab and get his order. He can eat when he comes."

Bertrand Gilson, New World's director of the board, was like certain species of apples — round, red, and sour, a circumstance I found perversely appealing. He was clever, despite his bluster and his air of discontent, and immensely successful. His achievements rested half on his own considerable gifts and half on his ability to spot talent and to manipulate it for his own benefit. Lunch with him was a singular event, and I could have considered my invitation as a reward for work well done; but I was not so foolish. Our tardy luncheon companion was the brightest of the company's hotshot chemists and one of the least prepossessing. I knew Gilson's tastes well enough to know that if McKenzie was coming, this confab was purely business.

Walter brought two fruit salads and a plate of rolls.

"Just start, Anna. Waiting for people is a bad habit. It interferes with digestion." He sounded cross, but his eyes were amused. Gilson and I shared a taste for eccentricity. Since I had realized that, certain things no longer puzzled me. Against all odds and common sense, Gilson trusted me, principally because, despite a host of superficial differences, we were the same fundamental type. We were both suspicious of conformity and capable of dealing with novelty. When Gilson had something awkward to handle, he called on me, a fact that was enhancing my career and eroding my stomach.

"Do you like turtle soup?"

"Yes, I do."

"We'll have the soup, Walter."

McKenzie began to look more important. I was getting the full treatment.

"You haven't asked me about this meeting yet, Anna. I assume you've checked up on our friend McKenzie."

"He's supposed to be our best chemist."

"That's what they tell me anyway. Ah, here's our young Einstein now." He gestured toward Walter, who escorted a pale blond man with a receding hairline, thick glasses, and a filthy lab jacket to our table. He looked like a back street doctor, and the hand he offered was stained with chemicals and nicotine.

"Philip McKenzie. How do you do?"

"Afternoon, McKenzie," Gilson growled. "Sit down and eat your soup."

McKenzie smiled beatifically, oblivious of the stares of the other diners, and rattled the test tubes in his jacket. "Perhaps I should take this off. We were running an interesting experiment."

He set a tube containing a disgusting brown concoction on the damask and arranged his jacket over the back of the chair. The fawn-colored shirt beneath was evidently his eating garment, because the relics of a good number of breakfasts, lunches, and dinners adorned its front. He pulled a shiny blue tie from his pocket and put it on, then, satisfied with his attire, proceeded with the meal at a remarkable pace, filching rolls from both Gilson and me before we could finish our share.

"Another helping, sir?" Walter asked.

"Oh, yes, please." Rumor had it that McKenzie lived in the laboratory, because the custodians kept finding food and bedding squirreled away in odd corners. That might be true: he ate like a man reduced to hot plate cooking. Gilson looked at me, then stretched his neck like a dissatisfied fowl. McKenzie must be worth a fleet of tankers.

"Finished?" Gilson inquired.

The chemist devoured the last few crumbs before Walter could sweep them aside.

"Yes, that was good, but I'd prefer a sauce with more body."

"I'll inform the kitchen," Gilson said dryly.

McKenzie sampled his coffee and lit a cigarette. "Did you read my report?" he asked.

"What I could understand of it. I want you to tell Anna exactly what happened in Frankfurt. Not the scientific aspects. She doesn't know any more about that than I do. That's your bailiwick. Tell us about the man — in detail."

McKenzie studied me for a moment, as if I were a compound with hitherto unsuspected qualities. "Right. I attended the big chemical fair in Frankfurt last month as a representative of New World Oil. I went with Dr. Orsini and Joe Sebastian as their advisor on certain scientific processes and patents. Nothing there. Waste of time." McKenzie wasn't the sort who enjoyed junkets and conferences. "There were also a number of seminars for purely scientific discussion, which I attended every day. At one of them I was approached by a man named Hermann Jaeger."

"Describe him for Anna," Gilson commanded.

McKenzie shrugged. "He was ordinary looking."

"Young or old?" I asked.

"Around forty, I'd say." Like many people with a gift for abstract thought, McKenzie was not overly observant. "He was fairly short, well built, had a crew cut."

I nodded.

"During the meeting, we had been discussing certain properties of fluids and the patterns of dispersion of one fluid through another. I had mentioned some of the theoretical implications of the work I've been doing for New World. As you may know, our unit is working on the ways various grades and types of oil disperse when mixed with water. Obviously there are important practical applications for this work."

"I understand."

"Anyway, Jaeger came up, introduced himself, and started talking. My German is excellent, incidentally. He asked me quite a few questions about what I did for New World, what my position was, and what the company was interested in at the moment, but I could tell that he wasn't a chemist."

"What was he doing there then?"

"Frankly, I thought he was trying to pick me up," McKenzie said with mischievous pleasure.

Gilson glared around the room at this remark; I considered the chemist's soft, rather delicate features and refused to be drawn.

"Go on."

"He invited me to lunch," McKenzie resumed. "I wasn't really interested, but he persisted. Well, what the hell, I thought, I was getting bored with Orsini and Sebastian, so I went. As soon as we left the hall, he began acting nervous. I asked what the matter was. He said he had something of great commercial importance to tell me. I explained that wasn't my field, but he said it would take a chemist to appreciate his information. We wound up having our talk in the zoo."

"The zoo?"

"Every visitor's supposed to go to the zoo, which is a perfect madhouse of tourists and kids. Not a bad idea. Once we got there, he relaxed and told me his brother's a chemist in East Germany. A very good chemist, apparently, because he had discovered a new process for the separation of oil and water — of oil and sea water."

McKenzie paused to let this sink in.

"What could this process be used for exactly?"

"Both for oil-spill cleanup and for the recovery of oil from bilge tanks. If his brother has devised a process as effective and as radically new as Jaeger claims, it would be worth a fortune, as well as having interesting theoretical implications."

"This could be enormously valuable for New World," Gilson said.

Yes, indeed. New World had gotten lucky at the patent office once before: it was the possession of certain drill component patents which had laid the foundation for the company's later growth. New World could compete with the big boys in only one area: technical expertise. If Herr Jaeger's brother was the real thing, and if New World could get him, there wouldn't be a tanker company or a seacoast country that wouldn't want our services. Very neat.

"What's the problem?" I asked.

"There are two," Gilson explained. "Is the man Jaeger genuine, and if he is, can we get his brother out of East Germany?"

"First things first. Did you believe the man?" I asked McKenzie.

"I don't know. He was very nervous. He claimed to be in considerable danger because of the business with his brother, but possibly he's only a con man. He was unwilling to reveal too much about his brother's work. That's understandable. Scientists working on the same problem often come up with solutions simultaneously without having had any contact. And, of course, after a certain amount of research, a seemingly minor piece of information may turn out to be the very thing that was blocking a particular line of investigation. I'll say this: he was believable as a nonscientist who has been carefully briefed by someone who knew what he was doing. Whether or not that someone is an East German chemist with a discovery, I can't be sure."

"And what does he want from you?"

"To relay his proposition to the company. If New World is interested, we make a preliminary payment in exchange for proof that the brother and his discoveries exist. Then, presumably, we negotiate with them and arrange the brother's safe arrival in the States." McKenzie lit another cigarette from the stub of his last one.

"How much?"

"Five hundred thousand dollars in Deutsche marks."

I looked at Gilson.

"I wish we knew whether Jaeger has approached any other company," he said.

"My guess," McKenzie replied, "is that he hasn't. Judging from our conversation, I have the impression that he investigated New World thoroughly. He hadn't been at any of the other meetings that I'd noticed, and he was so jumpy I don't think he'd have gotten through that routine more than once."

"But that's just supposition."

"That's why I asked for advice."

"There's a good chance we'll never see Jaeger again after turning over the money," I said, "so we ought to be sure he gives us something valuable right off. Something more than just proof of his brother's existence."

McKenzie nodded. "Jaeger claims that he has managed to get

a substantial number of his brother's papers to the West. He wants us to deposit part of the advance payment in a Swiss account. Then we're to meet him. I would be allowed to read over the papers, but not to remove them, unless he gets the rest of the money."

"What security does he have that we won't take his papers and leave his brother in East Germany?" I asked.

"If the work presented is of the caliber Jaeger claims, its creator would be extremely valuable — perhaps even more so than whatever process he has discovered so far, and I would assume that he would have committed only a portion of his work to paper. We might be able to reconstruct the entire process — would be able to, given time — but the man himself could provide it immediately."

"If he's genuine, then, he's gambling on the time factor."

"Right. It's a calculated risk, but if we pulled anything funny, the Jaegers could still try another company."

"How much could you learn from a brief examination of some technical papers?" Gilson wanted to know.

"In my own field — a lot. I would need time to think them over, of course, and to check out the mathematics."

"How much does Jaeger's brother get?" I asked.

"A percentage of ultimate profits and three million dollars — in marks."

"On the face of it, it's a bargain."

"That's what bothers me," Gilson said.

McKenzie shrugged. "There's the matter of getting the chemist."

"That's the other problem," Gilson agreed. "We don't want trouble with the Germans over this. Not with the way the oil and gas exploration is shaping up in the Baltic. We've got to be sure this Jaeger's going to be worth the effort. If we proceed, there can't be any slip-ups that expose New World involvement."

"That's not going to be easy, if Philip is evaluating the documents."

"We can cover that somehow." Gilson stared intently at the

scientist. "What's your opinion, McKenzie? We can afford to gamble up to a point. Do you think this is worth pursuing? From a commercial point of view, now, not a scientific one."

"I wouldn't have reported the incident if I hadn't thought Jaeger had something."

Gilson made up his mind. "All right. I'm turning this over to you, Anna. I think you and McKenzie ought to go to Frankfurt as soon as possible and meet this fellow. He doesn't get a dime until you do."

"He's not going to like that," McKenzie objected. "He planned to finish the deal with one more meeting."

"I'm sure he did," Gilson said dryly, "but for half a million he has to put up with some inconvenience. The delay will give us time to find out something about East German chemists. You'll get onto that, Anna?"

"Right. I'll get all the scientific directories and see if the computer can't winnow out some people with the right qualifications."

"Good. It's a priority."

I turned to McKenzie. "How are you to get in touch with Jaeger?"

"He runs a small camera store. To contact him, I'm to place an order for a certain type of lens. He will reply with the price and date it's to be shipped. That will indicate when he can meet me."

"And how will you know where?"

"He has a brochure illustrated with views of German cities which he uses to advertise his cameras. One will be enclosed. He will mark the place we're to meet."

"All very cloak and dagger," Gilson remarked.

"It seemed theatrical to me, but he insisted."

"Either he has reason to be afraid," I said, "or he hopes to add authenticity to the scheme."

"That will be your worry, Anna."

"How soon can the money be arranged?" I asked.

"We'll send it through the petrochemical works outside Cologne. I'll instruct Payments to work up a purchase order," Gilson replied. "A day or two at the most."

"Contact Jaeger right away, then, Philip, and better warn him it's to be a cash deal. I'll make the travel arrangements. Frankfurt is an important city for chemicals, isn't it?"

"Yes, they have an intensive industry."

"Good. Decide you need something highly refined, rare, difficult to duplicate — whatever. You're going to Frankfurt to buy it, O.K.?"

He nodded.

"I think, sir, the best thing for me is the petrochemical works. Sort of an inspection tour to meet the management, discuss the possibility of using Cologne as a base if we develop contracts for work in the Baltic or in the German sector of the North Sea."

"Good idea," Gilson agreed. "Is that all?"

"McKenzie and I can discuss the rest, and I will make some contingency plans if we decide to proceed with the chemist — what's his name?"

"Wilhelm. Wilhelm Jaeger. In English, it means William Hunter."

"Let's hope," Gilson said, "that the Jaegers' hunting is confined to chemistry."

Chapter 2

A LUSH MEDITERRANEAN FRAGRANCE greeted me at the door of our apartment.

"That you, Anna?" Harry called.

"Yes. What's all this?"

Empty tomato and tomato paste cans stood on the sink. Scraps of onions and peppers and garlic lay on the cutting board, while drips and smears of sauce adorned the fixtures as if Robert Rauschenberg had been working up a masterpiece in our kitchen. Harry was piling a plate with bread and cheese, interrupting his labors to stir an enormous pot of boiling pasta. As always when Harry played chef, the place was a wreck, but it smelled delicious, and I reminded myself that when I cooked and he cleaned, we ordinarily retreated to the hamburger joint. Domestic life is imperfect at best.

"Don't you remember? Jan's coming tonight."

"Oh, sorry," I said, kissing Harry, "I'd forgotten." It was already after six. "I'll go change."

"Don't bother, you look great. Were you meeting the brass today?"

"Yes. Full warpaint for a command performance." I kicked off my heels. "I'm getting out of uniform. Your friend Jan doesn't rate another couple of hours in this get-up."

"Don't you like him?" Harry asked as he took the salad out of the icebox.

"I hardly know him, do I? He seems a sharp operator, that's all. If you're going into business with him, keep your eyes open."

"You're too suspicious."

"I hope so, but be sure you have a lawyer go over everything before you make any decision. The fellow I told you about is the very best, and if he's busy, try my friend Brookie. She's young, but she works hard."

"You're getting as bad as my mother."

"Now and then even your mother gives good advice."

"At least you agree on something."

"We want you to be happy," I said, putting my arm around his waist. "I'd like to see you out of United Graphics and in your own workshop. You know that. I told you last year, I'd loan you the money."

"Chances are, I'd never have been able to pay you back."

"Nonsense. Your work's top flight. If it weren't, your buddy Jan Gorgon wouldn't give you the time of day."

"Then there's that lack of business sense my women friends all notice."

"O.K. On the face of it, Gorgon's a good idea. Just watch what you sign. He didn't get his mink and his Masseratti and all those admiring dowagers with pure innocence."

Harry made a face, then dived to rescue the spaghetti pot which was sending up fat starchy bubbles that broke and sizzled on the stove. I picked up my shoes and ran upstairs. When my last tenant left, Harry had agreed to give up his apartment, and we'd converted the duplex to one large house. Harry had done a lot of the remodeling and all the decorating, and I was extremely proud of the results. The kitchen upstairs had been combined with the living room to give Harry a studio, and one of the bedrooms was converted to a library for me. For furnishings, Harry had imported good Scandinavian pieces at what I originally regarded as monstrous expense. Once the bills were settled, however, I rapidly came to view my new luxury as mere necessity.

I opened the long windows, another of Harry's innovations. The magnolia's rustling patent leather leaves produced a feeling of contentment; I was a person who lived in a quite beautiful house in a neighborhood with room for a garden. Not bad, considering. The iron railing about the tree cast long, elegant shadows on the brickwork. Odd the power of possessions. Odd, because I spent much of my professional life examining possessions and evaluating what people were like aside from them. New World Oil's Research and Analysis Department: we found out who was worth what and whether Company X was as solvent as Company Y, so I knew possessions formed some of the world's most flattering mirrors and its most effective background noise. Maybe that's why I distrusted Jan Gorgon. His apartment looked like a seraglio and his gallery like a miniature Parke-Bernet. He owned an awful lot, and he made sure you saw it all. If he were an honest extrovert, he would do well by Harry, and sooner or later, his business acumen and Harry's talent would bring my friend a good return. If. And hopefully. It's a mistake to think artists need only spiritual rewards; they're susceptible to success, too.

The bell rang. I opened the closet, hung up the suit, escaped from the pantyhose, and pulled on a shirt and a pair of slacks. Sartorially, Jan would be resplendent enough for all three of us. He interested me; if I hadn't been anxious about how he might inveigle Harry, I'd have described him as a fascinating man.

Downstairs, Harry was setting the table, while Jan lounged in the foyer, talking. The dealer was all in white, with ultra suede slacks and a silk shirt of vaguely Cossack inspiration. Nearly as tall as Harry, he looked tough and fit, more like a rich athlete than a successful art dealer. Gorgon was the classic Polish type — wide, flat cheekbones, finely sculptured mouth, well-defined features. Some wandering Tartar had bequeathed him his faintly slanted eyes, and when he smiled he reminded me of a strong, smug, sensual cat. He could purr like a cat, too, when it suited him; and a great many of Washington's wealthy collectors had found that purr irresistible.

"Good evening, Anna."

"Hello, Jan. How are you?"

"Hungry. That smells delicious."

"You can thank Harry. My cooking is strictly in the survival category."

Jan laughed. "I've survived a lot of strange food. It left me with a taste for the best."

Maybe that explained him: the Gorgons had been refugees. He and his mother had gotten out of the wreckage in Poland after the war, fleeing first to Denmark, then to the States. He had once told Harry that he grew up in a DP camp. Like everything else with Jan, that was open to question, but he spoke Polish and Danish as perfectly as he spoke English, and he was fluent in French and German. From that linguistic competence alone, he must know a lot of things. I thought about the Jaegers and decided Mr. Gorgon might repay closer attention.

"Will you open the wine, Anna?"

"Sure. Just sit down, Jan. Do we need anything else, Harry?"

"A little first aid for some of these pots, that's all. I'll leave them in the sink."

Harry's a firm believer that whatever can be burned on can be soaked off, a fine theory if you don't mind dirty pans sitting about full of water.

"I'm serious about this deal," Harry said softly, "so be nice."

"If that's what you want, I'll be charming."

He grinned. "That almost worries me more."

"High class worries." I took the wine to the table and filled the glasses.

"I didn't know you were such a cook," Jan remarked. "This is excellent."

"I owe it all to the Army," Harry replied. "KP beats a lot of other duty."

"And the food is good, isn't it?"

Harry looked incredulous.

"When were you in the Army, Jan?" I asked.

"Never. I felt I owed that to my mother for getting me safely through one war. But I grew up on C rations. The first decent food I can remember came in a big brown cardboard box with U.S. ARMY stamped all over it." Jan helped himself to more spaghetti. "I've never wanted to try Army grub again, though. It might spoil my memories."

"I don't suppose you got deferred on those grounds."

Jan tapped his chest. "Touch of TB fortunately. The camp was full of it. You've got to know how to turn these things to good account," he said, and smiled.

"Harry told me you travel to Europe often. Does it seem strange to go back? Everything must look so different."

"Yes, mostly better. I was too young to remember much. Since I got into importing, I travel a lot."

"Importing artworks?"

"That's right. I started with Polish graphics. Very lucrative. The black market in art over there is fantastic."

"Don't you have problems with the government about that?" Harry asked.

"No. They want dollars, the artists want sales, and I want the product." Jan shrugged. "Something for everyone."

"The prints sell well over here?"

"They're first rate. The Poles turn out some of the best graphics in the world. Right, Harry?"

Harry nodded. "Jan's brought back some beautiful stuff."

"And sales. 'Art from the Captive Nations,'" he announced leaning toward me. "Do you like that? My first big pitch. Then I sold a package to a group selling bonds for Israel — 'The Dissidents Art Group.' Went very well. And then the Russians — beautiful stuff, you understand, but it needed packaging."

"And where were all these prints made?"

"Krakow and Warsaw; mostly by good Polish Catholic atheists. I don't ask about their politics, they don't ask about my sales pitch."

"No truth in advertising in the art world?"

"Ah, listen, Anna, you have the dealer, the artist, and the customer. The dealer I've got to take care of, because that's me. The artist I love. I love art, and the artist's got to live, right? The customer gets a good product and the illusion of his choice. After all the Philistines have the money."

"But do you ever purchase any work from countries besides Poland — from Russia or East Germany, say?"

"Why do you ask?" Jan's dark eyes were suddenly careful.

"Curiosity. A certain amount of stuff does get out, doesn't it?"

"Yes, of course. You read about the big exhibition in Paris last year? And there have been showings in New York. Naturally, it's bad to attract too much notoriety, but I've got a lot of contacts," Jan concluded mysteriously and changed the subject. "Has Harry told you about my proposition?"

"Just the rough outline. If you two want to discuss business, I'll go and do my share of KP."

"I'll help you clean up later," Harry said quickly. "I'd like you to hear what Jan has to say."

This was a sign of affection as well as confidence.

"Yes, please stay. Harry says you know a good lawyer."

"I suggested Lou Santos's firm. They specialize in partnerships and small businesses."

"Good. Now, what we want to do is to set up a workshop for graphics: lithography, silk screen, and woodcuts. We need a professional work place for artists in the Washington area. Something on the order of the old Tamarind workshop out West."

"We'd try to attract established people first," Harry added, "then train other artists in graphic techniques."

"I've had this idea in mind for ages," Jan continued, "but the problem was in finding someone with a reputation as a printmaker who also knew the mechanical processes thoroughly and who could actually direct and run a workshop. I've been trying to talk Harry into this for some time."

Which was why he'd hesitated about accepting a loan last year. "How long do you think it would take before this outfit showed a profit?" I asked.

"A while. In the long run, I'll make out all right because I'll buy up a certain proportion of the work."

"You can stand a tax loss, in other words."

"Everyone I know needs a tax loss, but Harry insists it be run for a profit. Artists are such capitalists. Until we're in the black I'll pay him a salary; later, he'll take a percentage of the gross."

"For motivation," Harry said.

"What about a building?"

"I think I've found the place," Harry answered. "I haven't even shown Anna this yet." He opened a Manila envelope and withdrew some photographs, a floor plan, and a sheet of specifications. Jan and I cleared a space on the table and Harry unveiled his discovery: a three-story brick-and-steel structure which had formerly been Kokpin Novelty, Inc. For the next couple of hours we conducted a thorough examination of its now gutted interior, while Harry explained how this bare shoebox piled with dust and rubble could be transformed into a workshop, showroom, and studios. The whole place would be cleaned, the old plaster stripped from the brickwork, and new floors laid. The lower floor would be left open to serve as a large printing shop. The second would be converted to a showroom, offices, and storage. The third would be outfitted to rent as combination studios and living spaces. He had several ingenious ideas for converting the building and for creating low-cost storage and living areas, and he had done his homework: he handed Jan long lists of materials and contractors' estimates. I found it impossible to visualize the metamorphosis of Kokpin Novelty; but both he and Jan were enthusiastic, and, from a practical point of view, the conversion of the old building looked to be something of a bargain. Afterward, while we were cleaning up the dishes, Harry asked me what I'd thought. I had to admit I'd been impressed.

He beamed. "If we can get the building, we're in business. It's a steal, because few companies can use anything that size in that neighborhood." He bent over the sink again and swirled hot water around a pan. "It's what I'd really like. United Graphics has lost its charm as far as I'm concerned."

"I know. I hope it will go through. And — you know if you and Jan need more money or if you'd like to put in something extra, that's no problem."

"Thanks, I appreciate the offer, dear, but Jan's being very generous."

"He can afford to be. Don't forget, you're saving him an architect's fee *and* a general contractor's fee."

Harry shrugged. I returned to the dishes. Some people give

an impression of complexity because they lead messy emotional lives: they're turbulent shallows. Others, like Harry, are complicated people with a deceptive simplicity of surface and manner. He was not "artistic," appearing serene, cheerful, down-to-earth; he could have been a hardworking teacher, plumber, carpenter, whatever; he had no "temperament." Everything important with Harry was hidden; it was only in his work or with rare things that he passionately wanted that one became aware of his emotions and artistic ambitions. This awareness was what had made me nervous about the venture with Jan Gorgon; independence from the thrall of United Graphics was one of Harry's cherished dreams, but one he would only accept on his own terms. I wanted him to get them.

"Admit it," he said, "you were quite taken with Jan, weren't you?"

"Yes, I was. He's certainly able, and you've told me yourself he's considered irresistible."

"I don't worry about that."

"I'm not sure that's a compliment."

"He's not your style."

"No? And what is my style?"

"Oh, rather less flashy, more substantial; someone less handsome but more sexy, someone — "

"Like you, for instance?"

"Very like me."

"Correct," I flung the dishtowel onto its rack and hugged him.

"What did I tell you?" he asked complacently. "But you seemed interested in him. Why was that?"

"I'm going to Germany in a day or so, perhaps to enter the importing business myself. It's a pretty wild story — I'll have to tell you about it."

Chapter 3

FRANKFURT AM MAIN announced itself with a roar of jack-hammers and power drills. The main concourse of the Hauptbahnhof was being gutted for a new underground line, and clouds of dust rose from the pit to engulf the tourists and shoppers, the business people and the fresh-faced American GI's crowding past the scaffolds to the bright, noisy plaza where masons were laying granite blocks for walks, benches, and flower basins. The duffel bags of weary returning troops lay heaped along the front of the building, while, on the plaza itself, their outbound compatriots debated maps and guides in soft Southern drawls and gazed at the raw bustling city across the tramtracks with a mixture of excitement and apprehension.

Temporary wooden catwalks funneled this pedestrian traffic to an underground passage connecting the Hauptbahnhof with the dozen or so tram and bus routes and with the line of hotels, businesses, and airline offices which provide a respectable façade for the decayed and sometimes dangerous red-light district behind. Although my hotel was only a couple of blocks away, I turned sharply to the right, skirted the plaza, and hailed a cab. The driver took my bag, but not the steel-reinforced black attaché case I was carrying. It had not left my hand since I had picked it up in Cologne a few hours before, and with good reason: I was carrying half a million dollars in Deutsche marks.

"*Guten Tag.*"

"*Guten Tag, Fräulein.*"

"*Haben Sie ein Zimmer für* Anna Peters?"

"Peters? *Oh, ja.* Sign here, Fräulein Peters. *Achtundfünfzig.*"

He handed me a key. "Fifth floor, Fräulein."

"*Danke.*"

McKenzie was at the same hotel. He had booked a room for

me when he arrived two days earlier for the preliminary meeting with Herr Jaeger. I had flown to Cologne the same day to meet with the management of the petrochemical works, tour the plants in the area, and discuss the possibility of a new office in the center city: useful — if nonessential — activity, designed to convince any curious observer that my visit was strictly routine. This morning, a complicated financial transaction with the home office completed, the manager of the petrochemical works had delivered the attaché case. As far as anyone else knew, I was in Frankfurt to pay a few courtesy calls prior to a return flight tomorrow.

There was time for a shower before I met McKenzie, and after locking myself and the attaché case in the bathroom, I set about removing the dirt and dust of the Bundesrand and of Frankfurt's construction. I had just finished when I heard a knock on the outer door.

"*Wo ist dort?*"

"Anna Peters?" asked an American voice.

"Just a minute." I scrambled into my clothes.

"It's Philip McKenzie."

I opened the door just far enough to identify him. "Hold on, the door's chained."

"Your German needs work."

"My Deutsch is merely a good will gesture."

McKenzie took in the large room, my bare feet, and my uncombed hair. "I'm interrupting."

"That's O.K. Come in." I fastened the door, then fetched the attaché case from the bathroom.

"Is that the money?"

"I picked it up today as we arranged. Have you contacted Jaeger?"

"He's all set. Can I see?" He gestured toward the case.

"What for?"

"I want to know what that much money looks like." His eyes glistened with curiosity. Perhaps McKenzie wasn't as wrapped up in fluid dispersal and oil chemistry as I'd been led to believe.

"All right." I took the key from the chain around my neck and opened the locks. There was an additional combination lock in the middle, set for the street number of Kokpin Novelty, Inc. The case clicked open: inside were neat envelopes filled with large denomination Deutsche marks. "Satisfied?"

McKenzie ruffled a few of the packets before I locked them away. "What's the plan for this afternoon?"

He turned reluctantly from the case, flopped into an easy chair, and fished a pack of cigarettes from the pocket of his tired green cardigan. I sat in front of the mirror, brushed my hair, and tried to observe McKenzie without appearing to stare.

"We're to meet Jaeger in the Palmengarten at four-thirty."

I nodded: a good choice. The Palmengarten was a *belle époque* botanical and pleasure garden, the pride of the city. I'd visited there and knew that almost anyone could be expected to show up for the afternoon concerts.

"He'll have a briefcase, too, and will join us on the terrace for a beer. We will exchange cases and examine them. If all's well, we go our separate ways."

"And you're sure you'll be able to determine if we've got the right goods?"

McKenzie nodded impatiently. "I told Gilson I could."

"All right; that's your department, just don't guess wrong. Assuming all goes as planned, what happens next?"

McKenzie paused to light a cigarette, carefully snuffing out the match before replying. "He will want us to prepare papers for his brother — so that he can enter the country on a priority basis and with an assumed name."

"That's *all?*" I couldn't help sharing my surprise.

"Jaeger says the rest is under control," McKenzie explained quickly.

"Let me get this straight: Jaeger is going to make his own arrangements about getting his brother into West Germany?"

"Yes — the money will take care of that." He gave the attaché case another fleeting glance. "Even the Socialist Workers' Paradise has a few people amenable to bribery."

"Undoubtedly, but my original impression was that substantial assistance would be required."

"It seems the Jaegers have developed other resources, contingent on their new wealth, of course."

"Of course." Gilson would be pleased: a flying raid across the Wall or a sprint for the border was the stuff of international corporate scandal. I was relieved, but oddly dissatisfied, too.

"Jaeger will let me know when and where to meet his brother — once the money has been deposited in his account."

"I think we must insist on meeting Wilhelm Jaeger before any payment is made."

"There will be difficulties."

"I think not. They will already have collected half a million — and gotten to the West. If they're confidence men, that should satisfy them. If they're not, and the brother really wants to work for New World he's got nothing to lose. He can always take his talents elsewhere."

"You're forgetting the time factor. His brother will need to leave Germany as soon as possible."

"We'll still have to see him first, Philip. You can discuss it with Gilson after you've seen the preliminary material, but that's my advice, and I doubt Herr Jaeger will be able to change my mind."

McKenzie shrugged and checked his watch. "Four o'clock."

"Do you have a car?"

"No. We can take a cab."

"Tram's as fast at this hour, more anonymous, too." I slipped on a pair of low-heeled shoes and picked up the case. "Ready?"

"Now or never," he replied with a nervous laugh.

On the Hauptbahnhof plaza we bought return fares at the machines and squeezed onto tram 8 with the rush hour crowd.

"Did you manage to get those chemicals?" I asked.

"Hmmm? Oh, yes, I did. Nothing I couldn't have gotten at home, but at a slightly better price. I picked up something for a friend of mine, too," he added, pleased.

"What's that?"

"A special high-power camera for lab work. It's for a kid I know. He came to the laboratory on one of those summer programs."

"Good student?"

"Andy? Potentially a brilliant chemist. This it?"

"Next one, I think. That sign's for the auto route."

"That's right." McKenzie took out a pack of cigarettes, looked at it and absently returned it to his pocket.

"Our stop."

"I should have remembered, but I haven't been here for a few years."

We walked half a block to the tall iron gate and entered the twilight years of the Hohenzollerns, where the Palmenhaus, its terrace restaurant covered with a cerise awning, faced a small, perfect lawn ornamented with a fountain and bordered by narrow beds thick with pink begonias. A peacock sauntered across the emerald grass, its iridescent tail repeating the shimmer of the rainbow over the water. The sun-drenched lawn and restaurant were set off by the shadows of treed arcades which led strollers to the gardens and the band shell or to the children's park, the grotto, and the boat pond. On the right of the Palmenhaus, a cheaper outdoor cafe with a buffet line and white metal chairs under striped umbrellas overlooked the freeform beds of ever-greens and cannas that bordered the lake. I found an empty table there and McKenzie fetched some drinks. The orchestra struck up a Viennese waltz; it was exactly 4:25.

"Damn bees," McKenzie said, brushing one of the yellow swarm from his beer.

"Hazards of eating in a flower garden."

He checked his watch and ran his eyes over the crowded cafe.

"Relax, this is tired businessmen's entertainment," I said as I watched the children feeding the swans. "I don't know about you, but this place makes me rethink monarchy and decadence. The Edwardians knew how to live."

McKenzie resumed his dispute with the bees, then broke off an assault and lifted his head sharply. "There he is, now."

A short, stocky man with a black attaché case was climbing the steps to the terrace. His round tanned face was coarse and unat-tractive, giving him the appearance of having been hastily, if solidly, modeled by some unthinking sculptor. He wore a plain brown jacket with a maroon vest sweater and a pair of brown slacks. At the head of the stairs he paused to survey the crowd before making for the buffet. Moments later, he returned with a cup of coffee and asked to share our table. He claimed the chair next to McKenzie, laying the black case beside mine. After a brief exchange of remarks in German, McKenzie announced that they would speak English.

"*Ja,*" Jaeger said, turning to me. "My English is quite good."

"I'm sure it's an improvement on my German."

Herr Jaeger laughed without sounding jovial. His round eyes were slightly bloodshot, but their expression was sharp. He did not strike me as nervous. Either McKenzie had projected feelings of his own onto Herr Jaeger or altered circumstances had renewed the camera dealer's confidence.

"Is everything in order?" he demanded brusquely.

"Yes — on our side."

"Good." He reached for my case.

"Of course, we want to examine your — merchandise."

"That may be done."

"Is there someplace suitable?"

"We have already decided," Jaeger said, rising from the table. "As we agreed, Herr Doktor?"

McKenzie rose and motioned for me to follow them. We descended from the cafe and passed before the ivy-covered Palmenhaus, its lower walls cloaked in three shades of begonias and decorated with urns of geraniums.

"A lovely spot, don't you agree?" Herr Jaeger asked me.

"Very."

"And the palms are interesting. They grow outdoors in America, don't they?"

"That's right: in California and Florida. Some are very tall — as high as that building."

"They would be interesting to see," Jaeger said politely.

A soft throbbing motor sounded behind the trees.

"Is that the train?"

"*Ja*, the *Kinderzug* — it's right on time." He smiled benignly as the miniature locomotive came into view and stopped to disembark a pack of fair, sturdy youngsters.

Across the tracks was a round sandy clearing with play equipment, largely deserted now that the breeze was blowing up and the brilliant sunshine fading into a cool and cloudy evening. Jaeger pointed through the surrounding foliage to a silver pond with three small islands, then we followed McKenzie around the playground and down the steep, stony path to the boathouse. He gave the boatman a coin, and the attendant drew one of the faded green rowboats against the dock. McKenzie stepped into the bow, Jaeger took the stern, and I was left with the oars.

"You can row, can't you?" McKenzie asked, as if this were a previously unconsidered detail.

"Let's hope it's one of those things you don't forget."

The oars were extraordinarily awkward, since, to prevent their loss, they had been nailed to the oarlocks. When the boatman released the craft, I pushed away from the dock to begin an erratic progress about the water.

"Avoid the other boats, please," Jaeger instructed.

We headed for the open water at the center of the pond. Jaeger passed his case to McKenzie and took mine, then steadied the oars until I could give him the key.

"The center lock works on the number it's last set to: four–seven–four–three."

Jaeger unlocked the case and held it, still closed, upon his knees. The pond was nearly empty, but he waited until we were clear of the small islands near the shore and safe from the two small boys rowing a collision course in an energetic tandem. Behind me, McKenzie was already shuffling through the papers Jaeger had produced; he had a slide rule with him and seemed totally absorbed. I backed water with one oar, then rowed slowly along the far shore, down the line of the barrier before the grotto and its waterfall, and recrossed the open stretch in the middle. The sun was behind the clouds, and I envied the men's jackets. For about fifteen minutes, we cruised in this manner, startling the oriental ducks and avoiding the shallows, the pipes for the waterspouts, and the grassy shore where, presumably, one or the other of my companions might attempt a surprise exit. Jaeger locked the attaché case with a snap and pocketed the key.

"*Ja,*" he said, "everything is in order." He smiled a faint, self-congratulatory smile and gave me an appraising look, as through considering whether I was the proper audience for this particular bit of cleverness. I glanced over my shoulder: McKenzie was still occupied, and, resigned to another turn at the oars, I maneuvered the boat once again around the fountain. Then for a time there was quiet. The waterfall was shut off for the night, and the deepening chill drove visitors back from the water to the rose-lined paths of the botanical gardens. The oars made a rhythmic, restful splash; the oarlocks creaked; children's voices floated over the trees; and, now and again, McKenzie rustled the pages he was reading. My hands were beginning to get sore.

Jaeger sat immobile, his elbows resting on the case, his tanned face looking more and more like a piece of battered terra cotta. I was struck again by the discrepancies between McKenzie's original report and the man in the stern. He exuded a watchful calm, as alert and confident as an animal on its own terrain. I turned the boat and searched the trees that screened the hill and the children's park: on the terrace fronting the water only two half-grown girls lingered to throw bread to the ducks; ahead, the empty grotto was engulfed by the shadow of the hill. Like a conjurer, the night wind had made the crowds vanish. Soon it would be too dark for McKenzie to read.

"I am convinced, Herr Jaeger," he said at last. "My congratulations to your brother."

The chemist's glasses caught the last glow from the pink clouds overhead. He nodded to me. "No doubt, Anna. The other people at New World will bear me out."

"I will contact you a week before my brother is expected," Jaeger said promptly, "to tell you where you should meet us. When we have the necessary documents, my brother will fly directly to America. I have already explained to Herr Doktor McKenzie what will be needed."

"If New World supplies documents for your brother," I replied, "we will have to be sure of his identity. Naturally, that assurance must precede any arrangements for transfer to the States."

Jaeger stared angrily at McKenzie for a few seconds. The oars creaked. "I do not like these delays," he snapped at McKenzie. "I thought our plans were understood."

"I don't control the money, Herr Jaeger," McKenzie apologized, with an anxious, resentful glance at me. I headed the boat toward the dock.

"You understand the danger to my brother, Fräulein?"

"I understand that we were talking about a great deal of money."

Jaeger's face was stern. "My brother's life is my first concern."

"There is no question of his being endangered. The sooner he reaches the States, the better, but if we are to turn over priority visas and all the necessary documents, we want to be sure whom we're getting. A brief meeting with Dr. McKenzie, maybe, then onto the plane. When your brother is safe in the States, he talks to our scientists and signs a contract, and you collect the money."

"That was not our plan."

"Dr. McKenzie didn't have the authority to make final plans with you." McKenzie was upset, but Jaeger, although obviously angry, did not seem seriously concerned. "You have no reason to worry," I continued, reassuringly. "Your brother will be in an even better position once he is in the States. After all, he will have his papers, his knowledge, a job — and if he's dissatisfied, there will be a score of other companies anxious to hire him. If anything, Herr Jaeger, we're taking the risks."

"It is a complication, nonetheless."

"Three million dollars produce a lot of complications."

"You say a meeting with Herr Doktor McKenzie?"

"Or one of our other scientists."

"With Dr. McKenzie: it must be someone I already know."

"All right — and me. Dr. McKenzie would not be able to handle the financial arrangments."

While Jaeger considered this, I shipped the oars and let the boat drift toward the dock.

"There must be no extra risks for my brother," he said at last. "You and Herr Doktor may see him when you deliver the passports and visas, but there can be no delay. Any evaluation of his abilities must wait until he reaches safety. Complete safety."

"We will have everything ready." I steered the craft toward the dock with one oar. The attendant grabbed the gunwale, allowing Jaeger to climb nimbly out. He was halfway up the slope before McKenzie and I left the boat, and by the time we reached the top of the hill, he had disappeared.

Chapter 4

"VERY, VERY INGENIOUS," McKenzie said as the cab pulled away. "A remarkable mind at work: opens all sorts of possibilities."

"I'm relieved to hear it."

"I'd had my doubts, too, but the man has a fine mind."

"His brother certainly seemed confident of his ability."

"Yes. A changed man, wasn't he?" McKenzie leaned closer and said in an undertone. "I really don't believe he thought it could happen — until I arrived the other day. You can imagine what it means to them."

McKenzie opened the attaché case to look at the papers, then resisted temptation, closed it, and lit a cigarette instead. "It will be interesting to work with him."

"I should think."

"Puts me in a new position, of course. I'm head of the team working on the problem, you know."

Which was why I detected a mixture of excitement and apprehension. "Yes, I knew that."

"We weren't far off — not if Jaeger continued on this line. Scientific discovery is like a horse race, though, speed pays."

"No doubt all his work will have to be replicated."

"Yes, our team will do that. I'm not worried about my job. Still — 'the invisible worm,' as Blake says: you have mixed feelings when someone else gets the credit."

"And the money."

"He'll be cheap at any price. The company'll make millions, billions, even. Scientists don't make all that much, considering the whole profit structure rests on scientific and technological discoveries."

"You guys aren't exactly sweated labor."

"Only in comparison to the ultimate value of our work. Look what athletes or entertainers make. We scientists are day laborers next to them."

"Labs cost money."

"Oh, yes, I'm resigned. Still, when you see a guy like our friend — tough luck he was caught on the wrong side of the Wall. Even what New World's going to pay him isn't enough."

"I hope you won't tell his brother that."

"No, just idle speculation; letting off a little tension, I guess. The excitement of it." He shook his head and fiddled with the case. "You have a strange job," he said without looking at me.

"Why strange?"

"Just peculiar — this sort of thing: traveling, making unusual arrangements."

"I'm an unusual person."

McKenzie gave me a sudden grin. "So am I. We ought to celebrate. Does that sound like a good idea?"

"Yes, I feel like partying."

"Good, but I've got to stop at the hotel first."

"We'll need to put the papers in the safe, anyway. I'll meet you in the lobby in half an hour."

As soon as we reached the hotel McKenzie relinquished the case, mumbled something to the clerk, then raced upstairs, leaving me with Jaeger's documents. Curious man: for some reason he was in a muddle of emotion, nervous and elated and apprehensive, all without losing the abstracted air which had distinguished him at our first meeting with Gilson. Despite his unconventional manners, he was strangely likable, and he worked easily with women, perhaps because he lacked any physical interest in our sex.

In fact, the business with Herr Jaeger had gone better than expected, although it was unfortunate that we'd have to deal with him further. I didn't trust Jaeger, I decided on the way upstairs. There was something peculiar about his manner, but his deficiencies would keep until after we'd consulted Gilson. Dismissing the Jaegers from my mind, I called Harry to inquire about the progress of negotiations for Kokpin Novelty, before donning a silk dress, high heels, and full warpaint for dinner; I'd had enough of hearty outdoor activity for one day.

McKenzie was lounging in one of the overstuffed maroon chairs in the lobby. Without really being "dressed," he gave the impression of having smartened himself up considerably. He wore a plaid jacket and a white shirt, and his chino pants, although shiny in the knees, were clean. He was now looking extremely happy with himself, and when he saw me, he rose and gave a comic bow.

"You're looking very sharp," he said.

"It's the company I keep."

He surveyed his garb with a trace of satisfaction. "I don't usually think about what I have on. Andy says — " Then he broke off and took my arm. "For a celebration, of course, I make the big effort."

"Where shall we go? I've had some good food in the Old Town."

"Would you mind if we ate here instead of going out?"

"Not at all, their food is excellent."

"There's some sort of delay about a call I placed to the States. I don't know why."

"The D.C. area? That's odd. I put a call through just a few minutes ago."

"Well, I've asked them to try again in an hour, so if you don't mind — "

"No, certainly not. You're the one who's been doing all the work — except for the rowing, of course."

"That must have looked funny, but there was no other way."

"It was a good idea, although conspicuous."

"According to Jaeger," McKenzie explained as we went downstairs, "hotels and cafes and such are under surveillance and the safest places are the most public, where nobody notices anybody else."

"He may be right. No one seemed to be following us in the gardens."

"No, I think it's all quite safe. Just nerves on his part. Ah, *danke.*" He picked up the menu. "Shall I translate this tome for you?"

"Just order me something good — chicken or veal but no liver dumplings or crazy-looking noodles."

"And wine?"

"Riesling, please."

"O.K. *Herr Ober.*" While he gave our orders, I looked about the restaurant, which was decorated like a wine cellar, with the broad whitewashed arches and black wood of the real thing. The sides of the rooms were lined with alcoves, each holding one or two tables. Around us were a foursome of ponderous-looking burghers settled in to some serious eating, a party of equally purposeful elderly ladies, a young family with a lively little boy, and a single man in a black suit reading the evening newspaper and nursing his digestion with mineral water. I kept returning to him. I had seen him before in the lobby: a soft, unimposing character with the bland, mobile face of a nervous blond rabbit.

"Which of us has he got his eye on, do you suppose?"

"Who?"

McKenzie nodded in the man's direction.

"Is he staying here — at the hotel?"

"I don't know. Don't tell me you're interested."

"I have the feeling I've seen him around. He's not eating much, is he?"

"Too many liver dumplings, probably. Or just a proper Westphalian businessman recovering from the wicked dissipations of Frankfurt."

"You sound as if you've covered that ground yourself."

McKenzie laughed.

"Do you know the city well?"

"Yes, fairly well. I studied in Germany, postdoctoral work in Heidelberg."

This led to a discussion of German towns. McKenzie had a surprising fund of anecdotes about student life, and a detailed knowledge of both the scientific community and the more raffish segments of German society. He was one of those individuals unable to resist allusions to things they wish concealed. This gave a certain coyness to his conversation, but his stories were more amusing than his scientific discourses.

"Would you like a liqueur?" he asked at the conclusion of one of these narratives.

"Not for me. Have one if you like."

Just then the head waiter approached: McKenzie's call had come through.

"Excuse me. I'll be right back. Order me a liqueur, would you? *Danke schön, Herr Ober.*" I watched him hurry up the stair; so did the man with the mineral water. I suddenly hoped that McKenzie hadn't done anything to make himself conspicuous in Frankfurt.

He was gone a long time. His liqueur arrived, and I settled the bill with the waiter. The man at the adjoining table grew restless, folded his paper, left. Finally McKenzie returned looking pale and miserable. He sat down, swallowed the liqueur in two gulps, and ran his hands through his hair, giving himself a wild, disheveled look.

"Bad news?"

He started, surprised to find me still there. "Family problems. I don't want to talk about them."

"I wouldn't ask."

He seemed to be debating how far he should confide in me. "I need a drink," he said at last. "Let's go somewhere and have a drink."

Now I knew how McKenzie had acquired his knowledge of nocturnal Germany. "All right. Let's do that."

We left the restaurant, and, even hurrying to keep up with McKenzie, I spotted the rabbity-looking man sunk in one of the soft chairs, his paper before his face. That was bad news, but I could hardly abandon the chemist, who was already heading down the Kaiserstrasse toward the Hauptbahnhof.

"Not down that way, Philip. Not at night."

Reluctant, he hesitated, then walked with me to a small beer hall in the Old Town, where I watched him find his way to the bottom of a couple of tankards.

"I can drink a lot of beer," he remarked unhappily.

"You ought to go back and go to bed."

"I don't get drunk easily."

"A seven-hour flight with a hangover is no fun, remember."

"I'd like some whiskey."

"What about trying the bar at the hotel?"

He nodded, but, instead of returning to the hotel, he once again set course for the Hauptbahnhof; and this time, I was unable to dissuade him. He had drunk just enough to be difficult, and the disadvantages of my lesser size and strength were unpleasantly obvious. I would have to wait until his mood changed or until he'd drunk enough to be lugged home. With the area fronting the Hauptbahnhof providing all manner of vice, that was not an attractive prospect. Within minutes, we found ourselves running a gauntlet of prostitutes, who, with their pimps and protectors, leaned against parked cars or hung around the doors of the sex shops, the cinemas, and the firetrap hotels that rent at four Deutsche marks the hour. Cigarette smoke and the sour smell of cheap liquor hung over the grimy street, and with them, palpable as the deafening music of the discos, a strange compound of desire and boredom, which some tastes find stimulating. We passed a group of nervous young GIs, and McKenzie, to my horror, accosted them. His proposals were made in fast, fluent German, but at least one of the soldiers was linguist enough to take offense.

"For God's sake, McKenzie! Come on."

"I was merely inviting them for a drink," he protested with exaggerated dignity.

"You've been misinterpreted, then."

For one of the soldiers had launched into a violent and profane tirade.

"Just a misunderstanding," I interrupted soothingly, pushing McKenzie out of his reach. "He's terribly drunk; has no idea what he's saying. His mother was buried yesterday. A terrible shock for everyone."

The other infantrymen murmured sympathetically at this and drew their buddy away.

"Don't start anything, Dave. She's got her hands full. American, too."

"What did he want anyway?" One of them laughed. "Sure got to you. Now if it had been the chick with him — "

The departing soldier yelled over his shoulder, "Get that fag the hell out of here, lady, before I knock his fucking head off." Good advice. "Let's go, Philip. You almost caught it there."

He gave a melancholy sigh, but refused to be steered to safer ground. He slouched through the unsavory crowd, ignoring the women in the tight shorts and high boots, the leather-lunged doormen bellowing the attractions of their particular entertainment, and the flashing neon lights and plastic accessories of the sex shops, as though he were homing in on some secret, but irresistible, objective. Two blocks later, this revealed itself as a dark, hot disco bar where strobe lights flickered like midsummer lightning. He squeezed into an empty chair and ordered two whiskeys. Around us gyrated a motley crew, most of whom had staked their turf somewhere between the sexes. McKenzie seemed sunk in gloom, drinking first his whiskey, then mine, and infecting me with his spiritless depression.

"Let's call it a night, Philip."

"No, no," he said, rousing himself, "people here we should meet."

"*Ist das nicht wahr?*" he asked the couple at the next table as an opener. His choice for companionship filled me with apprehension: a large, square, formidable middle-aged man and a tall, delicate boy with eye makeup, a flowered nylon shirt, and the lassitude of premature dissipation. It was the latter who attracted McKenzie's attention — to the entire disapproval of his companion.

"Philip, I don't think this is a good idea. Why don't you say good night."

The younger man had ignored McKenzie until I spoke. Now he turned and gave me a malicious smile. His eyes were peculiarly bright and sharp, like splinters of glass, and the pleasure of a little sexual rivalry had broken through his aura of drugged exhaustion. He shifted his chair and began flirting with McKenzie in a soft and surprisingly beautiful voice.

"This is going to cause trouble," I cautioned, but McKenzie shook off my warning. The older man fixed us both with a look of violent disgust and spoke sharply to "Uli," who ignored him. He called for more beer, and when the waiter brought it, gulped down a glass, wiping his mouth on the back of his hand between swallows. Closer examination confirmed my initial impression that I'd seen him on the late show. He looked fierce and Teutonic, his ill-fitting auburn wig only emphasizing the brutal contours of his impressive head. He started on his second beer, then reached out and jerked the boy around to face him. Uli did not seem distressed by this violent gesture, nor by the rough tide of invective which rolled after. He glanced over his shoulder, winked at McKenzie, smirked at me. Then McKenzie said something which caused the older German to stand up, knocking back his chair with a crash.

I pulled McKenzie to his feet. "We're leaving."

Uli's beautiful tenor shot over the thunderous music, before his companion lunged across the table, pushing him to the floor. A waiter advanced with a bouncer, but the dancers, scenting excitement, closed around us, cutting them off. McKenzie broke from my grip, and, keeping the table between himself and the Teutonic Terror with drunken craftiness, loosed a string of inflammatory remarks. I wished I'd let the GI flatten McKenzie earlier; he could have been safely back at the hotel nursing a black eye. Shoving my way to the exit, I ran into the street; no more than a half a block away were three men, recognizable even in mufti as American Army. They were alone and sober, and I asked them immediately if they'd like to help a compatriot in distress.

They declined my services, regretting they were broke. I took out three ten-dollar bills and explained the necessity of extracting a valuable scientist from the grip of the renowned Teutonic Terror. Two of them, country boys alert to the evils of strange women, hesitated. The third, a big city dude with lapels as wide as his shoulders, stuck out his hand and demanded twenty apiece. By now the sounds of the disco fracas were rising even over the drone of its sound system.

"Extortion."

He shrugged. "Wear and tear on the threads," he countered.

I handed over the cash, the company formed ranks, and we charged the disco.

"Which one?"

"Plaid jacket, white shirt, blond — there with the glasses." McKenzie was conspicuous, all right. He was the one dodging back and forth, while the Teutonic Terror advanced on him, simultaneously fending off the bouncers with one of the metal chairs.

"Who's the lion tamer?"

"The enemy."

"Got it."

We squeezed through the crowd, and the irregulars held a hurried confab. Then the two country fellows picked up a table and charged the Terror with a rebel yell, while their leader grabbed McKenzie around the neck and jerked him into the midst of the mob, yelling, "About face. On the double." I beat at the patrons before us with my purse as McKenzie was propelled toward the exit. In a rush, the other two soldiers brought up the rear, slamming the door on our pursuers' fingers. We were out on the street; and to the command, "Right face!" we marched smartly away, even McKenzie realizing the advantages of a quick retreat.

"Taxi, taxi!"

We piled in, McKenzie head first, and the soldiers locked the doors and rolled up the windows against the tardy assaults of the disco's bouncers and its more adventurous customers.

"*Schnell, schneller,*" I screamed to the driver, who floored the accelerator and took off with a jerk that sent us all onto the floor. Two blocks away, the GIs got out, received my congratulations, and shook hands all round. I gave the driver the name of our hotel, and, when we reached it, a sizable tip. McKenzie was not exactly a cheap date.

"*Kann ich Sie helfen, Fräulein?*"

"*Ja, bitte. Er ist —* " I couldn't think of a way to describe McKenzie's adventure in German. "He had too much to drink and — fell down."

The doorman nodded with the understanding born of long service. Inside, the combined efforts of two porters and a few random exertions by McKenzie himself brought the prodigal to his room. I pulled the drapes and began switching off the lights. McKenzie sat slumped on his bed. I was about to leave when he asked an unexpected question. "Have you ever been in love?"

"Couple of times."

"How did it work out?"

"Disaster once and success once."

"Disaster. The Greeks were right. A misfortune impossible to measure."

"Well — not all the time."

"Disaster," McKenzie said and shook his head disconsolately.

I left him sorrowing in the half dark and returned to the lobby, where, prompted by some instinct of good hostelry, the manager appeared. "Is everything all right, Fräulein Peters? Is Herr McKenzie all right?"

"Yes, thank you. He's not going to feel too well tomorrow, though, so I thought I'd settle the bill with you tonight."

"There is no rush, Fräulein, tomorrow will be fine."

"Dr. McKenzie will want to sleep as late as possible, so if you don't mind, I'd just as soon take care of everything now."

He went to his desk and prepared the account.

"Did Dr. McKenzie make a call to the States?"

"Yes, today and yesterday, too."

"I'll need to take down the numbers to make sure they're business calls. The expense account, you know."

"*Oh, ja.* I understand Fräulein."

It was a Maryland number. The main lab — or some friend capable of upsetting him so dramatically? "No other calls?"

"No distance calls. Local numbers are dialed direct from the rooms."

"Yes, of course." I signed the tab and gave the manager my credit card.

"Thank you Fräulein Peters. Come again. I hope you enjoyed your stay in Frankfurt."

I assured him that my stay had been memorable. It had. No matter what Gilson decided about the Jaegers, I knew there was some work cut out for me.

Chapter 5

I BARELY MANAGED to get McKenzie to the plane. Once aboard, he fastened his seat belt and, announcing he had work to do, immersed himself in a series of abstruse German scientific journals. The feckless conspirator and the self-destructive libertine alike had been banished: Dr. McKenzie was back to form, his passions scientific and his conversation nonexistent. His alcoholic pallor hinted at hidden complexities, but, throughout the trip, the scientist remained in the ascendant; and it was not until we reached Dulles that McKenzie made any reference to the events of the past days.

"Will you take this to the lab right away?" I asked as I handed over the case of documents.

"Yes, that will be safest. It will take time to go through everything. The senior scientists will meet tomorrow to begin a thorough evaluation."

"Good. I think there should be a copy made for Gilson, too."

"He'll get his tomorrow. I plan to report to him on the scientific findings as soon as possible."

"That leaves me with the rest."

McKenzie looked momentarily uncomfortable. "I don't have too clear a memory of last night, but I ought to thank you for keeping disaster within bounds."

"We needn't go into that."

"Thank you."

"But if and when we collect the Jaegers, stay off the sauce. We can't take any unnecessary risks."

"What will you advise Gilson?"

"I'm not sure. You say the work's first rate, but I can't help worrying about Herr Jaeger and his clever brother. I'm glad the final decision is Gilson's."

He nodded rapidly. "Yes, but I feel responsible for them and for their safety. They're committing themselves."

"I'll make that clear to Gilson, although moral obligations go only so far with him."

"But moral obligations with money are irresistible," McKenzie said, brightening at the thought. "I'll see you in a week or two, I predict, then back to Deutschland. Good-by until then, Anna." He shook hands and hurried to hail a cab.

The problem McKenzie himself presented was less easily dismissed. As soon as I had cleared away the most pressing business the next morning, I called the personnel office for his file, requested the records of the New World Summer Science Fellowships for the past five years, and consulted the numerical directory for the D.C. area. The number McKenzie had called from Frankfurt belonged to a fraternity house at the University of Maryland.

"Bess, has that material on the summer fellowships come in yet?"

"Not yet. Would you like me to get it?"

"Please — if you've got the time."

When she was gone I dialed the number. It rang a long time before a sleepy voice identified the fraternity.

"May I speak to Andy please?"

"Andy Ravelle?"

"Yes. Is he in?"

"Just a minute." He let the receiver drop with a crash.

"Naw, he's not in now. He's in labs most of the day. Any message?"

"No, I'll try again later, thank you."

Andy Ravelle. So. When Bess brought the material on the fellowships, I scanned the list: Oscar, Patterson, Pitti, Quinero, Ravelle. Andrew X. Ravelle had received a summer grant three years before as a high school junior. He had completed his project, which had a long and impressive title, and had been a finalist with it the next year at the National Science Fair. Not bad. I picked up the phone.

"Personnel, may I help you?"

"Anna Peters in Research. We had a student named Andrew Ravelle here on one of the Summer Science Fellowships, a high school kid. Do we have any subsequent records on him?"

"Just a minute. We did a follow-up study on that whole fellowship program. Ravelle, did you say?"

"That's right."

"Here he is: Finalist, National Science Fair, worked the next summer here under Dr. McKenzie — that was a special arrangement — not part of the regular program. Accepted MIT, transferred after his freshman year to the University of Maryland. Excellent grades in both institutions."

"Odd he'd transfer out of MIT."

"It says here 'summer study at the Goddard Space Center'— that's near Maryland, isn't it?"

"Yes, probably that was the reason. Let me have his address, please, home address, too, and his high school."

She gave me the data. Andrew X. Ravelle, schoolboy science whiz, fraternity brother, McKenzie's protégé, and precipitator of despair. I found him interesting, and even more so when I finished reading through his mentor's file. Dr. Philip H. McKenzie had studied at Harvard, MIT, Chicago, and Heidelberg. His résumé was full of prestigious degrees and awards, fat grants, and subsequently, fat salaries. All comprised an irreproachable record of creative and profitable work, except for the final items which were carbons of letters assuring three different lending institutions that Philip H. McKenzie, Ph.D., was indeed employed as a senior scientist at New World Oil's laboratory. They struck a small, soft, disquieting note: why was McKenzie borrowing substantial sums of money, the most recent from Friendly Loan, Inc.? Before the financial community could answer this interesting question, however, I was summoned to Gilson's office. There I spent a not entirely pleasant half hour recounting the German trip and attempting to delay a decision without admitting outright that I was worried.

"McKenzie says all the preliminary reports look excellent.

Dr. Orsini and Dr. Chiang agree — they sat up last night with the stuff. We won't hear from the Jaegers for a week anyway, you say. I don't understand why you're hesitating."

"You plan to go ahead with their visas, then?" I asked.

"Yes, that will be taken care of. You will prepare a brief supporting their request for priority visas as highly skilled workers and as political refugees. You should have that done today, no later."

"Very well."

"What is it, Anna? You ought to be pleased. I don't need to remind you how profitable this venture can be. What's bothering you?"

"I can't say at the moment, really, except I find it too good to be true. Jaeger appears, his brother's scientific documents are genuine. They can even make their own way to the West."

"Please don't forget what it's costing us."

"That's what bothers me. It's costing plenty and beyond what Jaeger's told McKenzie we don't know a thing about them. We haven't even been able to locate a likely East German scientist. I can't help feeling uneasy."

"You have to expect some problems in these matters. No gains without risks, you know." He tapped the desk slowly for emphasis. "I want this to go forward as soon as possible."

I could see there was nothing for it. "You'll have the papers this afternoon," I promised.

Gilson's orders kept me busy until after the banks had closed. I decided to call it a day — especially since I could tell his mind was made up. Then, on impulse, I got off the bus a half dozen blocks before my stop. Friendly Loan, Inc., was on the corner. I asked for the manager, who emerged wearing a denim leisure suit and sporting graying sideburns and a neat salt-and-pepper mustache. He had the bouncy gait of a man fighting to retain youth and a quick, irritable manner unlikely to inspire confidence in financial transactions.

"Bob Grimbala. What can I do for you?" he asked scanning my card.

"I'm investigating one of your customers, prior to a promotion for him. I wonder if I could speak to you privately?"

"Yeah, yeah. Come on in." He waved me into an office with a thick blue shag rug, a big metal desk, and a flashy nude splashed in pinks and reds. "O.K., make it snappy. Business picks up at this hour. Catch 'em going home. I got to get out there and keep an eye on the gals."

"This won't take long. Philip McKenzie, one of our senior research chemists, has borrowed money from this office. I'd appreciate it if you'd give me some idea of his credit standing."

Grimbala pressed his intercom button and ordered McKenzie's records. "What's he up for?"

"He's being considered for an administrative post overseas. It would involve financial responsibilities."

"And you want to know if he can keep his hand out of the till, huh?"

"To put it bluntly."

"Thanks Mabel," he said to the woman who brought in the papers. "McKenzie, McKenzie. He drummed a pencil against the desk, as he skimmed the contents of the folder. "Watch this guy."

"Why's that?"

"Look at his salary. He's pulling down close to 60 G's, right? No wife, no kids, no sick elderly. Rents an apartment I wouldn't be caught dead in, right? No large expenses."

"He should be pretty solvent."

"No way. Guys who are pretty solvent hit the local bank, huh? Sure thing. Your man's run out his credit with them; that means they think he's borrowed enough — even with his big salary and low overhead. I'll loan him up to a point, myself, that's all — he's got no assets to serve as collateral, see. Just his salary."

"McKenzie's not a typical customer, then?"

"Typical, not typical. All our customers need money — this guy's just got more to start with."

"What's he borrowing for?"

"Auto loan, college tuition for a friend." Grimbala shrugged. "If there's a good chance he'll repay, who cares?"

"A car — and tuition — that's what he said?"

"Sure. That's what the man said — more likely broads and ponies. Those two items go through a lot more dough than cars and colleges. Believe me. You should be in my position."

"It would be an education, I'm sure."

"You said it: I got my degree in human psychology."

"Thank you for your time, Mr. Grimbala."

"Yeah, you're welcome, and remember 'When you need a loan, be friendly, see Friendly.'" He preceded me to the outer office, "to keep an eye on the gals," as he put it. I imagined McKenzie sitting in his grubby jacket, fidgeting with his test tubes and studying Grimbala with a mixture of desperation and derision. I wouldn't have liked to be dependent on the good will of Friendly Loan, and was sure McKenzie hadn't like it either. I decided to have a look at Andy Ravelle.

When I inquired the next day at his frat house, Mr. Ravelle was in class.

"Then he'll be at the Chem Building all afternoon," one of his fraternity brothers explained. The brother looked as if he'd fallen from his bed to the door. Perhaps he was the somnambulist who'd answered the phone yesterday.

"I'm from New World Oil Corporation," I explained, "from our P.R. department." I reached for the bright enthusiasm of publicists without success, getting only, "They need a lot of P.R.," in response. My informant had a rumpled, malignant appearance and a faintly sour odor.

I tried again. "Ravelle was one of our Summer Scholarship Fellows — he won a National Science Fair award with the project he did for us. We've done a follow-up study on the recipients, and I've been assigned to interview some of them. I thought he'd be interesting."

"He is."

"Do you know him well?"

"No, but he's well known."

"Has a lot of class, does he?"

"Lotta cash."

"Generous?"

"Not him. Numero uno. But an Ornament of the House."

"I can imagine."

"Keeps us academically honest. Straight A's. Makes up for those of us less inclined." He coughed.

"You don't sound too well."

"Standing here in the draft doesn't help."

"Invite me in, then."

He thought this over, testing the quality of the proposition. He was tall and sallow, with a long, rather stupid jaw and a scrubby growth of beard. The upper part of his face was more promising: a fine nose and forehead and intelligent, disillusioned eyes. He was twenty or twenty-one at the most.

"Yeah, why not?" he said and stepped aside.

I entered a large reception room with elaborate plaster molding and a pair of marble fireplaces. Easy chairs and couches covered in oxblood leather stood in companionable groups on good, if faded, orientals, and the walls were adorned with photographs of sports teams, armored for football and lacrosse. Silver trophies dominated one mantel and a collection of ribbons hung over the other. In contrast to the brother in residence, the house possessed an air of comfortable semicolonial elegance, only slightly frayed by the rambunctious masculinity of its inhabitants.

"Very comfortable."

"Best house on campus. Nothing but the best for your prizewinner."

"Could take a photo or two," I said, remembering my role.

He made a face at this suggestion. "Care for a beer?"

"No, thank you."

He lit a cigarette. "Want one?"

"Don't smoke."

"I don't trust girls who don't smoke or drink."

"Grown women are a different matter." The hell with him. He gave a sudden, malicious grin. He was brighter than I'd credited. "My apologies, lady." Then he leaned forward curiously. "What do you want to know about Andy?"

"Has his family got money?" I asked, knowing perfectly well his dad was an apartment house superintendent.

"Never seen them."

"But Andy's got enough to throw around?"

"See that out there? The red phallic symbol? That's his. Costs him a fortune a semester in parking tickets. And skiing in Switzerland over the semester break and Italy this summer, I understand. No sweat for our boy."

"Who knows him well?"

"Every sorority on campus."

"Canvassing them would take too long. Anyone else?"

"Dr. Braff might know. He's his advisor."

"Where do I find Braff?"

"Chem building. Third floor." He checked his watch. "Probably in the lab now. Turn left when you go in."

"Thanks."

"Shall I tell Andy you came by?"

"That's up to you."

"I'll mention sometime that he's being pursued by an older woman."

"Pick the right moment," I said and opened the front door. Below the veranda Ravelle's car waited like a red torpedo. It had some of Mr. Grimbala's menace with a great deal more style. The chemistry building wasn't far away, and I located Ravelle's advisor without difficulty. Dr. Braff said he had a minute and invited me into a small office that smelled strongly of ammonia and acid.

"Take a seat, Miss Peters. You say you're from New World Oil?" Braff was a burly, cheerful man with a large nose and thick hands. His white hair and ponderous gestures suggested an inquisitive polar bear.

"We're doing a follow-up study on our Summer Fellowship Winners. Quite a few people have been doing the interviews, but I decided to look in on Andy myself, because one of my friends seems to think highly of him. Have you met Philip McKenzie? Andy worked an extra summer with him."

"Yes, yes, I have as a matter of fact. A very fine chemist."
Dr. Braff looked a trifle uncomfortable.

"He wanted me to ask how Andy was doing."

"Very well. A young man with enormous potential —
enormous."

"And how does he get along on campus? I imagine it's sometimes hard for such precocious students to fit in."

"If anything, Andrew fits in too well."

"Yet you said his work was good."

"It is, but he's given too much money, and I get the impression
he runs around too much. He can't keep that up. You can't
spend six hours in labs, make your other classes, and run around
half the night — not for long. But this is a big place, and students have to grow up here rather fast." He glanced at his
watch. "I have to get to my class now. Would you like me to
send Andy out for a few minutes?"

"When will the class be finished?"

"An hour and a half."

"Perhaps you could ask him to meet me then. I'll go have
lunch."

"All right. Nice to have met you." Braff escorted me to the
door. "You might — pass on what I said about Andrew to Dr.
McKenzie. He may have more influence with the boy than I
do."

He might indeed, but I doubted it, and my meeting with Andy
Ravelle confirmed my doubts. At first glance he was not exceptionally imposing: neither strikingly handsome nor ugly, just very
young, with pale, faintly olive skin, black eyes and hair. Although his graceful proportions made him seem taller, he was a
little less than average height. His features seemed curiously
familiar, and it took me a moment to realize that I had seen him in
a dozen galleries, for he had a face straight out of a Renaissance
fresco or a Roman frieze. Perhaps it was that faint suggestion of
timeless antiquity combined with extreme freshness which produced his charm, for he was undeniably attractive.

"Miss Peters? I'm Andy Ravelle. Dr. Braff said you had
asked to see me."

I explained about the follow-up study. His eyes registered

something when I mentioned McKenzie's name, but he just nodded at the end of the spiel and remarked politely that he'd been
grateful for the opportunity to work at New World. I wrote this
down; he was far too intelligent not to suspect any deviation
from the routine. We proceeded with the usual questions about
classes, colleges, future plans, and, since he was already far advanced, work in progress. He took my notebook and wrote out
the name of his current project in fat block letters.

"Anything else?"

"I think that will do it. I appreciate your time."

"Are you going back to Washington now?"

"Yes, as soon as I can find my car. I left it in that visitors'
lot — inconvenient to everything."

"I'll drive you over," he offered. The torpedo was now
parked prominently in front of the building. Andy unlocked the
passenger's side and plucked the parking citation from under the
windshield wiper. "I don't know why they waste their time," he
said, tearing it in half and letting the pieces float into the gutter.

"It's a beautiful car."

"Reward for good behavior."

"Did you deserve it?"

"That's not a polite question."

"The interview's over now."

"All right, then, no, I probably didn't. Does that suggest lurid
possibilities?"

"Mind boggling."

Ravelle laughed, and I have a feeling the conversation would
have become uncomfortable if a pretty blonde had not stepped off
the sidewalk ahead of us, waving frantically. Andy jammed on
the brakes and the torpedo settled back onto its haunches like a
well-trained cow pony.

"Hi, Mary Ann."

"Can I have a ride, Andy? I love your car. Oh, you've got
company," she said as though she had only just noticed. "Hi,
I'm Mary Ann Delibe. Isn't this a super car?"

I agreed it was admirable. She whispered something to Andy
and giggled. He shook his head.

"See you later. This is business."

He put the car in gear and we sped away.

"Girl friend?"

"She'd like to think so."

He smiled, then turned to wave at some other friends. I suddenly felt damn sorry for Philip McKenzie.

Chapter 6

AT TWO MINUTES BEFORE THREE that afternoon, an over-
loaded tractor trailer truck jackknifed across the southbound lanes
of the beltway into D.C., and, at three-twenty, I was breathing in
the noxious exhalations of a panting herd of stymied vehicles. It
was an appropriate end to a thoroughly depressing day, and the
ingestion of large amounts of carbon monoxide did nothing to lift
the gloom that McKenzie's private affairs had cast over our German adventure. Of the scientist's three interests — oil chemistry, Andy Ravelle, and money — two made him look unreliable
for the business in hand, although I could not have said exactly
why. There was no way, after all, that McKenzie was going to
profit from the importation of Herr Wilhelm Jaeger; quite the reverse. He stood to lose his premier position in the laboratory.
But his mercurial behavior in Frankfurt suggested that he had a
heavy emotional investment, not only in Ravelle, but in the
Jaeger connection as well. Whether or not there was a relationship between the two affairs, the fact remained that the negotiations with the Jaegers and conversations with Ravelle both sent
our top chemist into high gear. Then there was Ravelle himself.
Innocent youth corrupted by affluent sophisticate? On balance, I
thought not. If anyone was being corrupted, it was probably
McKenzie, who appeared to have made a fool of himself in the
most extravagant manner

Still, even Ravelle might not mean too much. Everyone's affairs went through less than halcyon days, and I was weathering a
bit of domestic unrest myself at the moment, which encouraged
me to take a philosophical view of McKenzie's difficulties. My
trouble, in a word, was Kokpin Novelty, Inc., which was turning
out to be encumbered with a dismaying variety of liens, loans,

and legal entanglements. Harry, serene in the face of physical danger, emotional upheaval, artistic risks, and most other human calamities, was panicked by lawyers, paperwork, and red tape. The week before his income tax was due was perennially an ordeal for all concerned, and the ideal print shop location was turning out to be a legalistic nightmare beyond anything the IRS had so far devised. I had been steering a course between feigned ignorance and unwelcome meddling with indifferent results. Combined with my apprehensions about McKenzie and Gilson's push to get the Jaeger brothers as quickly as possible, Harry's current venture made me think a return to Germany might be positively welcome.

With this in mind, I stopped at a phone booth in the city and called Jan Gorgon. He was leaving the gallery for the day and asked me to come to his apartment, which occupied the townhouse adjoining his showrooms. Even though I had been tempted from the first to sound him out on the German business, I had not seen him since the night we studied the plans for Kokpin Novelty, having resolved to avoid anything that might smack of interference. I was uneasy enough now to abandon that resolution.

"Nice to see you again, Anna. Harry says you've just come back from Germany. Did you have good weather?"

"Yes, thank you. Sunny every day."

"Come on in."

I followed Jan through the short hall to his living room. Whatever modernist impulses ruled his gallery, none was in evidence here. There were masses of fine prints on the walls, along with a tiger skin and some Turkish rugs. The thick beige carpet struck a restrained note underfoot, but the rest of the room was a riotous collection of antiques and *objets d'art*, all of prime quality but so crowded together that one had less the sense of a conventional room than of some eccentric sorcerer's cave, crammed with his talismans and fetishes and overhung with his banners. The windows, closed with old-fashioned dark wooden blinds, increased this not unpleasant feeling of mystery. Gorgon might have been an old India hand returned with his trophies or a silk route trader surrounded by his wares; the latter, most probably, for he was dressed in a white burnoose with handsome embroidery, a garment which he wore with perfect aplomb and which suited his flamboyant style completely.

Jan sat down, swung his feet onto an odd little table supported by a ceramic gargoyle, and waited. I decided to come straight to the point.

"Do you remember the night you came to dinner, when I asked you about your importing business?"

"I remember you seemed rather interested."

"I'd like some advice — off the record."

"I keep lots of secrets," he said in the dramatic undertone which doubtless sent his dowager customers into flutters of excitement.

"This case is hypothetical. I just want to get your reaction." I outlined the proposition the Jaegers had made to us. Jan listened intently, and, when I was done, raised his eyebrows and made an odd clucking noise.

"I don't like it, although anything's possible. Can we assume that this scientist is connected with the petroleum industry?"

I nodded.

"East Germany pumps oil from Russia, for refining. Comes into Halle. So Halle, Magdeburg, or Dessau. Right in the center of the country." He thought this over, and shook his head. "Someone with the capabilities you've hinted at would almost certainly be well known. Assuming for a moment that he isn't an old man, he'd have been trained under the present regime. Certainly they'd know what they had in him, and, you know, most of the technical people are loyal. They don't defect too often. Why should they? They've got a good deal already."

"There's always the exception."

"Just be sure this is."

That was something to think about. "But, assuming we have a dissatisfied scientist, how does he get out?"

"Their scientific people travel, attend conferences. For that matter people have just run across the border, sailed out of East

German waters, even stolen planes. Not what I'd recommend, though."

"No," I agreed. "Suppose there's a lot of money available?"

"Well, it wouldn't be a matter of bribing a border guard to look the other way."

"I had imagined something considerably more elaborate — and expensive."

"Expensive is correct. The pros charge around twelve thousand dollars to get someone out," Jan said casually, one finger tracing the embroidery on his robe. "But it's by far the best bet if you can afford it. All very routine and businesslike. The good ones have excellent records."

"I see."

"Better yet, if there's money enough, would be a false identity which would enable him to pass legally to the West. That would square with what you've said about the emphasis on secrecy. Otherwise he would be safer with a splash of publicity — a celebrity defection makes good copy."

"Is defection the right word when one's financially motivated?"

"I don't know. In theory, you'd think that would make him the most reliable from our point of view — politically reliable, I mean," Jan laughed.

"You've lived in Washington too long," I said.

"No, I have traveled too much. Much too much."

"Anyway, your conclusion is that it doesn't smell right."

"It may be perfectly all right — most refugees have stories no one would believe. I know I do. But be careful."

"I will. Thanks, Jan."

"Anna — "

"Yes?"

"I think you could be looking for the wrong things in this."

"What do you mean?"

"Well, your efforts have been directed at determining whether or not this man is a con artist, right?"

"Yes, that was my thought."

Jan shook his head. "Look into his politics. Look in East

Germany — not literally, keep out of there — but find out who this man is and what he thinks."

"We're trying, but the name is obviously a false one, and, even with the computer, investigating the dozen or so guys with the right jobs and the right age ranges is rough. I'm afraid we'll have to commit ourselves before we have any definite results."

"Good luck, then, but remember what I said. If he's the real thing, he's an exception."

A cheerful thought. Jan was right. All things considered, New World Oil ought to tell the Jaegers to seek asylum in West Germany, offer them a position through our company in Cologne, and forget any cloak-and-dagger business about whisking Wilhelm and Hermann straight to D.C. I would recommend that to Gilson tomorrow, and then McKenzie could contact Herr Jaeger before he made any final arrangements. By the time I unlocked our front door, I had settled on this plan.

"Hi. Anybody home?"

"Hi." Harry's voice came from the kitchen, followed by an angry clatter of dishes. I looked at my watch. I was later than expected, and I suddenly remembered that it had been my turn to do the shopping. The day was certainly running true to form.

"Any news?"

"I should ask you," he said crossly.

I shrugged. Harry was in a touchy mood, but so was I. "All right, sorry I forgot the shopping, but you don't need to snap my head off. I was out at College Park all afternoon and got stuck in the traffic jam. You must have heard about it on the radio."

"You weren't at College Park at quarter of five."

So that was it. He must have passed Jan's apartment and spotted my car. "No, I stopped to see Jan on the way in. I wanted to ask him — "

"I know what you wanted to ask him. I never realized how incompetent you really thought I was until this business."

"And I never realized how self-centered you are. I am sick to death of Kokpin Novelty, and, as a matter of fact, I went to ask Jan a few questions about East Germany."

This was not the nicest rejoinder, and Harry and I spent the next few minutes embroiled in one of those sudden emotional storms that discharge the accumulated frictions of domestic life. I brought it to an abrupt halt by stamping upstairs and slamming the bedroom door; under certain circumstances few sounds are as satisfying as the reverberations of a casement. I changed my clothes, washed up, consulted the magnolia, and was on the verge of admitting that I was getting hungry, when Harry tapped on the door.

"Come in."

"Dinner," he announced with a perfectly straight face, "is served."

"Bunter would say, 'Dinner is served, my lady.' "

"Bunter doesn't throw titles around loosely. When you get a title, Bunter will announce it with pleasure."

"For his sake, I will do my best to acquire one."

"An event gratifying to all concerned, I am sure."

I broke up. "You ought to have gone to Hollywood, Harry."

"Too tall. I'd make a super butler, but I'd be bigger than the leading men. Robert Redford would have to stand on a ladder to get his coat on."

"And then starlets would be running off with the butler before the end of the flick."

"Not much chance of that — unless his temper improves."

"There's nothing wrong with his temper that fewer lawyers wouldn't cure."

"That's for damn sure."

"Come on, then, Harry," I said, hugging him, "give the strong silent type a rest. You're entitled once in a while, and I get tired of having all the crises. Tell me the latest on Kokpin Novelty, and I'll let you in on what I found out today. And no advice from either of us."

"A deal. But dinner is still served."

On the way downstairs, I remarked that I liked Jan. "I was wrong about him."

"Oh?"

"He's a sensible man. You should leave the lawyers to him."

"See, you can't resist," Harry replied in a warning tone. "That's advice."

"A thousand pardons. But I'll be forgiven when you hear the story I've got. By the way, what's for dinner?"

"Eggs. Eggs are what happen to people who forget the shopping."

"Now," I said, "I feel properly penitent."

For a man of so determined and individual a personality, Bertrand Gilson had left remarkably little imprint on New World's standard executive suite. My original mentor in the company, Henry Brammin, had fought the canons of the functionalist school with considerable ingenuity. Over the years he had managed to convert his particular glass-and-steel box to something resembling the solid mahogany and brass offices favored by magnates of a much earlier era. In comparison, Gilson was more amenable to the dictates of corporate taste. He had, of course, seized the best of the more luxurious suites and arranged it to maximize his convenience and to minimize the comfort of subordinates summoned before him. That was only to be expected. Personal touches were, however, limited to the obligatory family picture and to a drilling core mounted in chrome and lucite, which stood against one wall. Aggressive — even eccentric — as Gilson might appear in person, he did not often ruffle the smoothness of the corporate hierarchy. His chosen decor confirmed that observation and increased my uneasiness: he was about to go along with corporate pressures and to reject my carefully formulated advice regarding McKenzie and the Jaegers.

"Yes, yes, that's right. You arrange it with Miss Braun." He pushed another button on his phone. "Amelia? Take care of Carl Ivor on that stock deal. And no more calls.until I'm through here."

He hung up the phone. "Sorry about the interruption. Now, where were we?"

"Travel arrangements."

"Yes. Well, as I said, you and McKenzie will go directly to

Cologne to see Jürgen Honiss — you've met him. He has a home outside the city. Supposedly, you will be staying there for consultations with him. He will provide a car, and you and McKenzie will drive from there to wherever you are meeting the Jaegers."

"Who arranged this?"

"McKenzie discussed it with Jaeger."

"McKenzie's showing a considerable talent for intrigue."

"Neither McKenzie nor I credit Herr Jaeger's notion that East German agents have him under surveillance. If they did, he would hardly be so confident about getting his brother to the West. But once Wilhelm Jaeger's safe and sound and once the word gets out that he's got a patentable process, the competition will swarm. Therefore, everything must be done as quietly and efficiently as possible. And that is why your suggestion, Anna, that we keep Dr. Jaeger and his brother in Germany is unthinkable."

"I've explained my reservations about the Jaegers. It doesn't look as if it will be possible to determine the scientist's real identity, not within the time span. We're getting all sorts of special exceptions made to bring the man here and put him into our labs without having any idea who he really is or how he is managing to leave East Germany. I think the company's taking a big gamble by not paying more attention to the possible repercussions."

"Frankly, Anna, if Dr. Jaeger brings the expertise we want, all that is irrelevant. I agree with McKenzie. We have made an arrangement with the Jaegers and we should carry it through as planned. He had a signal from Jaeger this morning: you two will leave tomorrow, and you will be notified about the meeting place once you're in Germany."

The situation had gotten out of hand even faster than I had anticipated. I was provoked to say, "I cannot believe, sir, that the corporation would approve of this venture."

Gilson's face grew dark with anger. "That is where you are wrong. Several of the most important of our directors are extremely interested."

"They've been told?" This seemed highly irregular.

"The matter of obtaining the new process was raised briefly," Gilson said sharply and, I thought, a trifle defensively.

"But surely not how we hoped to acquire it?"

Gilson leaned back in his chair and swiveled it so that he could stare out at the cerulean sky. "Crystal Blythe called me about the matter last night."

I understood now why he had been unusually patient. Disaster had called — particularly for me.

"She had gotten wind of the plan."

"Not through McKenzie?"

Gilson shrugged. "Several people knew by this time. He's one of the possibilities."

"That in itself should be reason for treating him with extreme caution."

"I don't need you to point that out." He let his chair snap forward in irritation. "You and I are in an awkward position with Crystal. If we don't go ahead, she will raise the question at the next meeting of the board. In view of the percentage decline in profits over the last two quarters, she could make a very embarrassing case out of our failure to move aggressively."

"But you are still her trustee — you control her shares and you will for another three years." I knew that, because I had secured the agreement with Crystal under highly unusual and unpleasant circumstances. Barring some spectacular corporate upheaval, my tenure with New World Oil would end the day she took control of the Blythe family holdings.

"I am scarcely looking to retire in three years."

So Crystal Blythe was as formidable as ever. Even I hadn't supposed she'd tackle Gilson quite this soon.

"That is why you are flying to Germany, tomorrow, and why you are going to return with the Jaegers and their scientific process. There is no question about it."

"Perhaps Crystal would feel more confident if I were not included."

"On the contrary, she felt your presence was essential."

Yes, no doubt. A success was a coup for all concerned; a failure, the pretext for the elimination of two people who'd gotten the better of her. Gilson had overreached himself when he'd held onto her shares and now he'd let himself be out-maneuvered.

"It seems to me, sir," I said, rising to leave, "that you've put the noose around both our necks."

Chapter 7

JÜRGEN HONISS drove us home in a black BMW. The house, an impressive wood-and-brick construction in sight of the Rhine, confirmed my notion that he had made a good thing out of his post as manager of New World Oil in Cologne. Honestly, of course: Honiss had an air of solid, old-fashioned business integrity, courteous, if a trifle dour, straightforward, and efficient. On previous occasions I had found him pleasant and easy to work with; this time I sensed a certain constraint. Large transfers of cash through his office, mysterious communiques, and now the reappearance of McKenzie and me spelled irregular dealings, abhorrent to his nature. It seemed to me that I was corrupting a member of a simpler and, on the whole, more admirable species, an impression intensified by meeting his family, as tall, blond, and handsome as our host. Brimming with health and affluence, Jürgen, Inge, and their children were living advertisements for the new Germany.

After dinner with these paragons, we walked out on the lawn overlooking the river. Low, powerful barges were still plying the current, bilge water pouring from their vents, flags stiff in the evening breeze. On the far shore, the brick buildings turned to copper, then vermillion; while in the distance, the woods and fields of the Rhinepark sank into deep green shadow. The Honisses' slate-colored Great Dane tore about the grass, while McKenzie led Helga and Dieter, the two youngsters, on an expedition down to the river. McKenzie was unexpectedly good with children, his cold, abstracted demeanor evaporating in their presence. While we watched them romping below, Inge described a new American exhibit at the Wallraf-Richartz Museum, and Jürgen walked slightly behind us, saying little. Finally, commenting that it was getting cold, he asked his wife to see about coffee. I turned to follow her, but he stopped me. "A moment, Miss Peters."

Inge left, and we admired the view.

"Yes," he said in response to my compliments, "this is a beautiful section." He smiled without enthusiasm and produced car keys. "Here. It's in the garage, a Mercedes. Full tank of petrol — everything you need."

"Thank you."

"The car has been rented for two weeks by a brother of one of my assistants," he continued. "I hope that will be all right."

This meant, of course, that he hoped McKenzie and I were not up to anything too disgraceful. I said the arrangement seemed satisfactory.

Honiss went on relentlessly, "As far as anyone else is to know, you and Dr. McKenzie are staying with us?"

"That's correct. I hope it won't prove awkward for you. If we get a message tomorrow, the business will be wrapped up fairly quickly."

This prospect made Jürgen look even gloomier, but further conversation was prevented by the approach of the children, who raced McKenzie up the hill to arrive in a state of great hilarity. Jürgen smiled, relenting a little, "The children would be content if Herr Doktor stayed behind."

The postcard was delivered the next morning. It was waiting beside my place at breakfast, a few inches of shiny Agfa-color showing a plaza centered with exuberant fountains and encircled with benches and flowers: the Karlsplatz in Munich. On the reverse was the date and time for our meeting with Jaeger, and, a day later, McKenzie and I pushed through the crowds along Prielmayerstrasse. As in Frankfurt, excavations were under way for a new subway line, and the barriers and catwalks added to the already considerable congestion. There was noise and dirt and a press of street vendors that reminded me of New York. And like New York, Munich sported a cosmopolitan population: Bavarians in *Lederhosen* and collarless loden jackets jostled British and Italian tourists; Swedish hikers with knapsacks and climbing axes passed Turkish immigrants; while salesmen and entrepreneurs of every type and nation squeezed along the scaffolding toward the Karlsplatz. The morning's drizzly rain had ended as we started out, but the smell of damp and soot lingered in the air.

"What time is it?" McKenzie asked.

"Quarter of."

"It has a lower level, you know."

"We'll find him."

We entered the stairs for the underground passageway to the plaza. Below were shops and a great variety of food stalls, which provisioned the crowds standing around high tables drinking beer and coffee and soda and gobbling pizzas and sausages.

"Hungry?"

"No, I don't think so." McKenzie seemed nervous and excited.

"Better eat anyway. Buy me a bratwurst, would you, and I'll get us some coffee."

"Do we have time?"

"Of course — it'll look better, too."

"All right. That's an idea." He went through his pockets in a distracted manner, until I conceded defeat and handed him some change. I had already learned that regardless of his expense account, any loose Deutsche marks vanished into McKenzie's reserves, never to reappear.

While eating lunch, we took a turn around the lower level without spotting Jaeger.

"It's noon," McKenzie said. "We'd better go up to the plaza."

Above, the postcard materialized. The Karlsplatz was a semicircle fronting a complex tangle of tram- and buslines. The wide, circular basin in the center was its dominant feature, along with the clouds of spray that shot up from the ring of water jets set in the rim. The backdrop for the whole business was a curving row of tall hotels, restaurants, and offices, punctuated in the center by the elaborate carved gate to Neuhauserstrasse, which runs from the elegant shopping area to the Marienplatz. Every bit of seating on the plaza was filled, even the granite blocks about the fountain, producing the impression that the hostels of the country had suddenly discharged their inhabitants into the center of Munich. Amid all this footsore youth, Jaeger was not to be found. McKenzie and I made a circuit of the plaza, then laid claim to the edge of one of the raised flower beds. A few minutes later, a man in a brown suit sat down on the other side.

"Have you brought the documents, Fräulein Peters?"

"I have yours."

"And my brother's?"

"You know our arrangement."

"It will be dangerous for my brother to delay any longer."

"I hope we can all leave for the States tomorrow, but today Philip and I must meet him."

I rose and started walking toward Neuhauserstrasse, McKenzie and Jaeger following on either side. We passed under the pale gray arches of the Karlstor, entering a pedestrian mall ornamented with flowers. One side held an arcade leading to further restaurants and shops, and there were ice cream vendors and fruit and vegetable stalls. I bought some ice cream cones, and when I handed Jaeger his, I passed him the special entry visa he needed. He slipped the document into his coat pocket.

"The other one, too."

"I didn't bring it."

Jaeger turned to skirt a small, but noisy, political rally, which shared an open section of the mall with an itinerant magician. Two women were passing out leaflets, and an intense, unshaven fellow in a dark coat began to harangue the bystanders. McKenzie paused to listen.

"Come on," I said, disliking the incomprehensible enthusiasm of the crowd.

"Then," Jaeger resumed, "there's the matter of money."

"We're not going to discuss that."

"There have been unforeseen expenses."

"For us all," I replied, "but you've gotten enough already for any reasonable arrangements."

Jaeger nibbled on his cone. "We will leave here separately to avoid suspicion. You will come to meet my brother, then we will discuss the money."

"We can discuss it. There is no possibility of your getting more at the moment."

"I think we must be flexible on this," McKenzie interrupted.

I didn't bother to answer him. "Where shall we meet you?"

"We have rooms over a small beer hall on Nymphenburgerstrasse. You cannot miss it if you take the tram from the Hauptbahnhof — number four or twenty one." He glanced at McKenzie who nodded rapidly.

"I know the area," he said.

"Good. The beer hall has a garden in front. At the side, there is a small entrance. The stair on the right leads up to the apartments. Knock twice at number ten. We will expect you within the hour."

Jaeger pitched what was left of his ice cream into a trash basket before disappearing through the arches of the arcade.

"It's possible they do need more money," McKenzie remarked as we walked toward the station.

"For what?"

"Pay off someone who may have spotted the brother. Jaeger did insist he was being watched in Frankfurt."

"We're not working for King Midas, you know. Our friend's going to have to manage on what he's already gotten. I could stretch that much pretty far and so could you, I imagine."

"We don't want to lose him at this point. There are other oil companies."

"You're pushing awfully hard, Philip. Just be careful you don't go too far."

"What do you mean?"

"I mean that I have a lot of reservations about this deal, and the more you push it, the more I wonder what's in it for you."

"For me — for the company. It's the chance of a lifetime."

"I'd say the question is for you or for the company?"

"There's the tram," McKenzie replied, ignoring this remark. "Have you an extra ticket?"

*

The beer hall fronted Nymphenburgerstrasse. It was a three-story white building with a garden where numerous patrons were braving the dank air to drink under blue-striped umbrellas and ramshackle awnings. Out front a shriveled little man with an accordion did his best to sustain their resolve. As McKenzie and I walked toward the beer garden from the tram stop, it struck me that the Jaegers had chosen a curiously commonplace hideout.

"There's the door."

"Let's walk around the block first."

The street behind was quiet and perfectly respectable. The Jaegers' building abutted a large apartment house, next to which stood one of the Bavarian state offices. If there were another exit, it was probably through the beer hall or the garden. McKenzie and I returned, mounted the stairs, and knocked. Almost immediately, Jaeger opened the door and motioned us into a large nearly empty room. As I had supposed, their apartment occupied the corner of the building, enabling them to watch the entrances to both the flats and the beer hall. There was a chair by each of the windows, probably for that very purpose, and a bed against the back wall. Wilhelm Jaeger was sprawled on the latter, smoking a carved pipe.

"Es freut mich sehr, Sie kennenzulernen, Herr Doktor," McKenzie said, shaking hands.

I studied our *Wunder*chemist while they exchanged pleasantries. Wilhelm Jaeger was, I guessed, older than his brother, perhaps forty-five or even fifty. He was bigger, too, although built along the same square, sturdy lines; but the chief difference — as well as the main similarity — lay in his face. Like Hermann, he had thick, almost ill-shaped, features, but his were part of an altogether more impressive design. His dark eyes were exceptionally forceful and intelligent. If Hermann awakened doubts because he looked like a capable thug, Wilhelm appeared at once more imposing and more ruthless. He had a firm handshake and an undeniably magnetic presence. It was entirely possible that he was, indeed, a chemist of extraordinary ability as well as a man ambitious enough to betray his country's interests to further his own.

"I do not speak English, Fräulein," he said slowly.

"*Ich spreche ein wenig Deutsch. Sprechen Sie Deutsch mit Herr McKenzie*," I replied and took a seat on the other side of the room. There was an awkward pause during which a good deal of sizing up occurred on both sides. Wilhelm Jaeger struck me as being a formidable man; this was both good and bad. It was likely that New World would indeed get the genuine item; it was also likely that dealing with him might be more complicated than we had anticipated.

McKenzie produced a notebook and began to put some technical questions to Wilhelm. I turned to his brother and asked if there had been any problems.

"A few. I had been watched in Frankfurt. That is why I made this arrangement."

I glanced out the window. The street below showed nothing suspicious. "Is there another entrance?"

"There is a fire escape leading to the garden."

"You have gotten proper passports?"

He nodded. "There is a need for more money, though, Fräulein."

"You have gotten a sizable advance already. As soon as your brother signs a contract with New World, you will get your money."

"It is not so simple as that. It will not be possible for us to leave right away."

"And why not?"

"I have business to wind up."

"Surely you trust your brother."

"Even in the States, my brother will be in continual danger, especially once his identity is known and once the process becomes public knowledge."

"I can assure you that New World will not be careless with someone as valuable as Dr. Jaeger."

Hermann waved this aside. "My brother was able to secure many of his papers."

"What are you offering, Herr Jaeger?"

"We are offering you the process in return for our money, deposited as planned in a Swiss account."

"I would have to get special authorization — and our senior scientists would have to evaluate the work."

"You do not trust Herr McKenzie?"

"In science, most things are double-checked."

"Others might not be so cautious."

"That is the chance we must take. We have already been very generous."

"Obtaining the process is more important to your company than getting my brother."

"Yes, agreed. And simpler, too."

"Very much."

I thought this over. The offer had certain definite attractions. "I would have to consult with my company."

"We could give you another day."

"And we would have to see the papers before we made any cash transfer."

"Let us leave it this way, Fräulein. Talk to your company. If it seems safe enough for my brother to leave Germany, he will. Otherwise, we will exchange the papers for the cash. Is that satisfactory, Herr McKenzie?"

He spoke sharply, causing McKenzie to turn with a start. There followed a rapid conversation in German. McKenzie seemed taken aback by this turn of events, and he argued surprisingly vigorously. At last Wilhelm Jaeger broke in. *"Morgen,"* he said, "tomorrow." There was no doubt that he was a person of considerable authority, and at last McKenzie agreed to whatever had been proposed.

"We are to meet them tomorrow," he translated, "in the Englischergarten. If the material on the process is complete, you will telephone the home office and set the arrangements in operation. If we do not agree, they will meet with Royal Dutch. The preliminary contact has been made."

This was what we'd feared. "What do you think, Philip?"

"We must go ahead. We have no choice," he said, upset.

"You don't sound confident."

"I have no doubt that Dr. Jaeger will have the process," he replied firmly.

"Very well. When are we to meet you?" I asked Jaeger.

"The papers are in safekeeping. We will meet you tomorrow at two. Walk up from the Haus der Kunst on Prinzeregenstrasse. Take the path that runs parallel to the stream. We will spot you."

We agreed to this, turned over Wilhelm Jaeger's priority visa, and left. On the way back in the tram, McKenzie complained of nausea, blaming the bratwurst he'd eaten. He did, in fact, look rather green.

"Don't expect me for dinner tonight," he said as we reached the hotel. "I'm going to spend a quiet evening in bed."

"You don't have any doubts about Wilhelm Jaeger, do you?"

"No," McKenzie said with a slight shiver, "none at all."

With this, he retired to his room, and I began a complicated series of transatlantic telephone calls to Gilson. When I got off the phone sometime after seven, everything was in order for our transaction with the Jaegers. I stopped on the way to dinner to knock on McKenzie's door; he said he didn't want anything. Maybe his indisposition *was* the bratwurst, but when I returned, I thought of something else. I asked the desk clerk if he spoke any English.

"A little, Fräulein."

I gave him a ten-mark note. "I'm here on business for my company with Herr McKenzie in room eight fifteen." The man verified this fact and nodded. "Herr McKenzie is a brilliant man but an alcoholic — he *trinken* too much."

"*Ach, ja, ja,*" he replied sympathetically.

"He gets himself into trouble."

"*Kampfen?*" He gestured with his fists.

"*Ja,* and other problems. I am here to prevent — *verhüten das.*"

After further pooling of our linguistic resources, he promised that if McKenzie left the hotel I would be notified at once. With this precaution, I went upstairs, took a shower, and stretched out on my bed for a couple of hours with a paperback. I had decided to forget McKenzie and switch off the light, when the phone rang: Philip had left the hotel.

"In welcher Richtung?"

I understood only one word of the reply, *"Hauptbahnhof."* I dropped the phone and ran to the window. By squeezing onto the narrow balcony, I managed a glimpse of McKenzie. He was turning down Bayerstrasse. I grabbed my coat and keys, raced down the back stair and out into the street. McKenzie, of course, was no longer in sight and at the corner, I assessed the situation. The station? Unlikely, somehow. The main entrance was, in any case in the opposite direction. There was no sign of him on Bayerstrasse. That left the Karlsplatz. I took off toward it as fast as I could go.

I spotted him near the underground walkway. He had on a dark raincoat, which like most of his wardrobe was loose and rumpled. He seemed to be carrying something — a small package or a book, but I could not be sure; and although there was still a fair number of people on the street, I didn't dare get too close. He paused momentarily at the top of the stair to the Karlsplatz, sending me hastily into the doorway of a large department store, where I nearly compromised myself with a drunk who spoke Italian. Below ground, McKenzie crossed swiftly to the other side; so he was not heading for the trams. I let several people ahead of me on the escalator, then followed, emerging into the breeze that carried spatters from the fountain as far as the steps and wafted a misty spray over the pavement. The sky was a murky pink and the full moon hung over the Karlstor like a Japanese lantern. McKenzie hurried through the gate. I was more and more puzzled: this did not look like the prelude to one of his typical dissipations.

Along Neuhauserstrasse, the cafes were still busy, and the night was mild enough for sitting out in the metal chairs on the mall. McKenzie ducked under the shelter on the right hand side, then entered the arcade. I went after him, stopping at the door of the large cafe. He was nowhere to be seen. Behind me, a few strollers were still admiring the toy display and the model planes. I checked the street on each side, but there was no sign of

McKenzie. He had, either intentionally or not, given me the slip in a most professional fashion. I bought coffee, went through the cafe again, then sat outside courting rheumatism — still no Philip. After three quarters of an hour, I retired to the hotel, where the deskman informed me that Herr McKenzie had returned, none the worse for wear, some twenty minutes before.

Chapter 8

WE TOOK THE U–BAHN to Odeonplatz, then walked through the Hofgarten toward the "English Garden," a large wooded park which, my companion explained, actually honored an American Colonial. McKenzie related the story with the conspiratorial excitement familiar from Frankfurt. I had been quite wrong, I realized, to suppose that his controlled, work-obsessed personality was the norm. Rather, he seemed to be a person subject to wide swings of mood. Work provided a framework to counterbalance this tendency in his nature, but on off-hours like our junket, McKenzie's temperament had full play.

He had joined me for a late breakfast that morning, arriving just as I was finishing my tea.

"An unexpected decor," he remarked.

The hotel, solidly conventional — even stodgy — throughout, revealed another spirit in the breakfast room. A vast collection of leggy and rapacious plants cluttered the window ledges and swarmed long poles to catch the sun. A cage of twittering canaries was suspended amid the foliage at one end, a companion cage of parakeets at the other. The breakfast tables, themselves unexceptionable, were paired with an eccentric collection of stuffed, half-stuffed, and unstuffed chairs of considerable antiquity. Around them, the walls were hung with souveniers, chiefly painted plates, cuckoo clocks, and other Bavarian wood specialties. An umbrella stand filled with peacock feathers and another jammed with dried reeds completed the effect of rambunctious clutter.

"I rather like it."

"Yes, I get sick of all that everlasting tidiness."

"How's the bratwurst today?"

"All right."

"Did you get out for something to eat?"

"No," McKenzie said. "I went right to bed. *Danke, Fräulein, Kaffee, bitte.*" He took the boiled egg the waitress had given him and sliced off its top neatly.

I wondered how informative he felt that morning. "How well do you know Hermann Jaeger, Philip?"

He shrugged. "Not at all, really. We've talked quite a bit, but just arrangements."

"I mean, had you met him before Frankfurt?"

McKenzie looked up. I had pushed the warning buzzer. "Why do you ask?"

"They threatened us yesterday with Royal Dutch. I thought it was odd that they hadn't gone that route in the first place."

McKenzie buttered his toast.

"Hermann is certainly a cool enough character to have approached two or three firms — despite what you said about his nerves."

"Yes, well, it might have been awkward to explain to Gilson. To tell the truth, I met him a couple of years ago on vacation. I was rather at a low point then."

"Like our last night in Frankfurt?"

"I'd been having a lot of problems, personal problems."

"I thought maybe that was it."

"Unnecessary to go into all that with Gilson."

"Unnecessary. Unless you know something important about Herr Jaeger."

"What's wrong?"

"Something's worrying him. Did he say anything — about being followed here, anything like that?"

"Not in so many words."

"He's not the type to be easily rattled."

"Not at all. Nor his brother, either. I was impressed by him."

"Me too."

I was tempted to ask McKenzie where he'd been the night before, but resisted. Our meeting with the Jaegers was apt to be tricky enough without an argument beforehand. Just the same, I was sorry I'd lost him along Neuhauserstrasse: like most people who deal in half truths, McKenzie was hard to figure.

The Hofgarten ended at a lawn set off by a somber screen of poplars. A grim and curious monument, half in ruins, rose in the center with a granite block and a sunken pool, now empty, before it. The building was of dark gray stone, surmounted by a dome and fronted with a facade of pseudo-Byzantine designs on a faded gold ground. There was no sign of life except for the shrubs that had begun to grow from the dome, and the building looked like nothing so much as a set for some elaborate Eastern opera. On the far corner of the lawn, a young couple in raincoats stood in an oblivious embrace. They gave the composition a poetic touch which Harry would have appreciated.

"What's this thing?" I asked McKenzie.

"Some sort of military museum — Nazi era, I think."

If so, Munich had found an interesting way of dealing with what was now a historical embarrassment. Harry would have found that worth notice too. He'd been on my mind — he and the negotiations for Kokpin Novelty. I hoped that we could get the papers from the Jaegers and go home soon. It was not often that Harry needed moral support and even less often that I was in a position to be a soothing influence.

"This way," McKenzie said. "This walkway takes us under the traffic circle to the garden."

We entered a well-lit subterranean passage. I looked back over my shoulder.

"Someone behind us?"

"No, just a touch of claustrophobia."

"Women are supposed to like enclosed spaces."

"Says who?"

"Shrinks and psychologists."

"A lot they know about women."

"Not a believer?"

"They make enough to take cabs, anyway."

"Don't worry. Not many muggers here. Rocker gangs, though."

"What is a Rocker gang?"

"Black leather jackets, bicycle chains. Might be quite an adventure."

"I was thinking of the Jaegers, actually."

"They said they'd meet us in the park."

"Don't be too trusting, Philip."

"My life story." He looked unhappy, and once again I wondered what sort of emotional stake he'd had in Dr. Jaeger's discovery.

The passage sloped gradually upward to emerge next to the modern art gallery. Beyond were the trees of the Englischergarten. I opened the map I'd bought: one of the trails ran beside the stream that fed the museum pond. A few toddlers were feeding the ducks on the bank and some old women sat, half dozing, on the benches near the water. Ahead lay a wide meadow edged with shade trees, and, along the stream, a woodland. As McKenzie and I started up the path, few other people were in evidence.

We hadn't walked far before a line of riders emerged from the strip of woods — fifteen or twenty of them. They came out in single file and trotted in a big circle on the meadow, to the dismay of several large dogs that had been frolicking on the grass. McKenzie and I stopped to watch.

"There's a riding school up off Königstrasse," he explained.

The riders cantered into a figure eight. After a few more maneuvers, they returned to a trot and formed a double file, evidently headed for one of the dirt riding trails which laced the park. They had started to cross the roads ahead of us when there was a commotion in the brush. The lead rider pulled up her mount sharply, as a big dark bay crashed out of the bushes, hurdled the stream, and tore into the line of riders, spooking the horses and almost unseating several pupils. Blocked by the nervous mounts of the riding school, the bay circled, flinging its head about in panic, foam dripping from its mouth. We saw then that a rider was sprawled across the horse's neck, his feet still hooked in the stirrups. The riding instructor spurred her pony and caught the runaway's trailing reins. The bay reared in terror, tossing the man backward onto the ground and dragging him as it shied away. Someone screamed, but the damage had already been done: the front of the man's riding habit was soaked with blood. The bay's neck dripped red, too, and there were dark spatters running down the saddle.

McKenzie ran forward, ignoring the horse's frantic lunges, to seize its bridle so that the riding instructor could dismount and bring the animal under control. The class spent a few minutes in noisy ineffectuality, before one of them galloped off for the police, while others disentangled the corpse. McKenzie and the riding instructor led the trembling horse away, then he returned to stand near me on the asphalt, wiping his scarlet hands on a handkerchief. A man in a tweed riding jacket pushed past us to bend over the body. When he rose, shaking his head, I saw the dead man's face. His riding cap had fallen off to reveal pale blond hair. Below was a soft face, much paler now than it had been in the hotel restaurant but clearly recognizable. He'd been stabbed to death, and no matter who he was or where he came from, that meant trouble of the worst sort.

"Let's get out of here, Philip."

"We're witnesses. The police will be here in a minute."

I drew him back from the growing circle around the body. "Don't you recognize him?" I whispered.

McKenzie started to wipe his face, noticed the blood on his handkerchief, and dropped it. "No, I — just acted automatically. The horse — " he said, and stopped.

"He's the man we saw in the hotel in Frankfurt — the man with the newspaper and the mineral water. The one who was watching us. Probably the one who'd been keeping an eye on Herr Jaeger."

I thought for a moment McKenzie might faint. "We've got to find them," he said, his face ashen. "We must talk to them right away."

"I doubt they'll still be around — not if they got wind of this business."

McKenzie swept around the fringes of the group and headed for the trees. "Quicker this way," he said. "We'll get the U–Bahn near the edge of the park if we don't see them first."

A green police car was closing rapidly on the scene. McKenzie and I crossed a bridge and gained the shelter of the trees.

"Let's wait here for a few minutes," I said, stopping him.

We left the path and climbed a little hill in the wood. I stood on one of the benches at the top and peered down through the foliage. From the edge of the park, the swings and seesaws of the children's playground gave out a monotonous grating screech. Drawn by the sound of the cruiser and the ambulance, several of the children's mothers had already begun walking toward the road, and some of the riders were moving cautiously into the brush under the direction of a patrolman. Had the Jaegers been anywhere near the scene they would surely have departed by now.

"No chance of them still being here."

"We've got to find them." McKenzie rubbed nervously at his bloodstained nails.

"The main thing is to keep clear of this mess." I jumped off the bench and almost stumbled. Delayed reaction. McKenzie looked pretty shaky too.

"We can connect with the tram for Nymphenburgerstrasse," he said.

I decided to save discussion for later. "Let's go back for the car instead. We should leave Munich as soon as possible."

"The Jaegers," McKenzie said, shaking his head. "We must get those papers."

"The Jaegers will be leaving, too. I think that can be guaranteed."

McKenzie looked startled. He mumbled something unintelligible and set off rapidly for the park gates. I wasn't sure which was more surprising — his courage in the face of a gruesome killing and a terrified horse or his panic over the loss of the formula. On the way back downtown on the U–Bahn, he seemed completely absorbed by this scientific mishap, leaving me to consider the nontechnical implications. I thought that the best we could hope for was that the pale rabbity man was a notorious East German agent with an immense number of enemies. That was the best — that and the hope the Jaegers had somehow been kept from going to the Englischergarten. The worst possibility was very bad indeed. Contemplation of how disagreeable things could get convinced me that New World Oil should forget the Jaegers' scientific discovery. I hoped I could explain that to Philip, but once he'd absorbed the incident in the park, I didn't believe he'd need much persuasion. *I* certainly didn't.

At the hotel, we packed our things, and I signed for the rooms, McKenzie, as usual, being engaged elsewhere when bills were to be paid. I told the manager that I would leave my bags for a moment and get the car.

"Herr McKenzie has gone for the car, Fräulein."

"He's already come down?"

The manager pointed to a case behind the desk. "He said he'd meet you out front. I'll help with the luggage, Fräulein. Ah, here is Herr McKenzie, now. Careful of the traffic."

He loaded the cases into the trunk.

"Do you want me to drive?" I asked. McKenzie's driving was sometimes alarming.

"After we get out of the city. You don't know Munich."

"All right." But I knew Munich well enough to know we weren't heading for the autobahn. "Wrong turn," I said.

"Right turn. You don't think I'd leave without seeing the Jaegers, do you?"

"If the Jaegers had nothing to do with the business in the park, they have nothing to worry about. We can go back to Cologne, and they can send another card to Honiss."

"And suppose they're in trouble — suppose that man getting killed attracts attention to them? We can't just leave them."

"Can't we? The Jaegers got West O.K., and even by the least generous estimates they should still have the better part of half a million dollars with them. And the man who was following them is dead. I think they can take care of themselves — a lot better than you and I can."

"If that man was an East German agent — "

"What if he wasn't?"

McKenzie turned to look at me. A tram bell rang furiously, and he stamped on the brake, throwing me against the dashboard, but avoiding the crossing where a bright red tram whipped by. McKenzie seemed scarcely to notice.

"Do you know how long I have worked on this problem?" A horn sounded behind us. The Mercedes stalled; McKenzie restarted it.

"Ten years," he said. "For the last ten years I have lived and breathed oil chemistry."

"This is a little different. We're not going to a scientific conference. I'm not sure you understand the risks yet."

"And you don't understand the potential of what the Jaegers have."

"I understand they could have had that man killed. That's what I understand."

"I have spent ten years," he repeated. "We must get those papers — not for you, not for New World, but for me. It is absolutely essential."

McKenzie sat slightly hunched over the wheel. He was very white, but he seemed totally resolved, as impressive in his own way as the formidable Jaegers. There was no doubt that he could call on unsuspected resources. I wondered how long they would last.

"Do you understand, Anna? I am not joking. We will do whatever is necessary to get those papers."

"You will do whatever you think necessary. I will do what I think sensible. And I control the money. The Jaegers get nothing unless I release the funds."

"If you do not, I will call Gilson and explain your refusal."

"Will he take your word against mine?"

"He will have to. Unless we get that patent, he's going to be out. Something about head office politics, but I know it's a sure thing."

"You've done your homework."

"I had to. And isn't it worth a chance?" he asked, conciliatory now. "We'll go to their apartment, we'll make a deal with them — they may be willing to settle more quickly after what's happened. Please — "

"How much is in this for you?"

There was a long pause. "Not a lot," he said finally.

"I don't believe you."

"All right. One hundred thousand. Why shouldn't I have it? Their work is genuine. I can guarantee that."

I wondered how: I had a few ideas — all unpleasant.

"How much do you want?" He sounded desperate.

"Half."

"That's too much."

"Let me out at the next light then."

"All right. Don't touch the door."

"That buys you one visit to the Jaegers. If we don't settle with them this afternoon the deal is off, and we go home."

We passed the beer garden on Nymphenburgerstrasse and started around the block. McKenzie was a quick learner.

"This is how we play it," I said. "We were held up on the U–Bahn — a breakdown or something. When we got to the park, we saw an ambulance and police cars — people running all over, so we assumed that the meeting was off. Understand?"

"Yes, that's good — if they believe us."

"They'll believe us so long as it suits them. We're on our way to the airport — that's why we have our luggage. We will offer to take them with us."

McKenzie nodded. "And if they agree?"

"They either weren't in the garden or that man was an East German agent — or both."

"And if they don't?"

"Then I think we're in trouble."

Chapter 9

M CKENZIE PARKED DOWN THE BLOCK from the beer garden, and we walked back to the side entrance. The shades in the upper apartment were drawn, suggesting that the Jaegers might already have decamped. I stopped McKenzie halfway up the stair.

"What is it?"

"Are you very sure you want to do this?"

He didn't brush off this inquiry but considered for a few seconds as though I had posed some scientific question, intelligible, yet tricky to explain.

"Perhaps I should tell you," he said, "I've undertaken something rather ambitious."

"Last night? When you went out?"

"You knew about that? That was the climax, so to speak. The height of folly."

I had an idea what was coming, but its exact shape still eluded me. "The Jaegers do not have a scientific discovery."

Unexpectedly, McKenzie smiled; solutions delighted him. "Clever Miss Peters. The Jaegers *did* not. Now they do. I gave it to them, and we must get it back, before they're tempted — "

"To sell New World's patent to another company?"

"To sell *my* discovery to another company," he corrected.

"One you made in our laboratories."

"I'll still only get a fraction of what my work is worth, you understand."

"How could you conceal it? You worked with a team of chemists."

"I faked some of the results, enough to throw them off the most promising track. Usually scientific fakery is done the other way. No one anticipates results being made worse."

The rumors about McKenzie's unconventional living arrangements made more sense; his nights in the lab had simplified the operation of his plan. "I see."

"No, you don't. Only another scientist would see what I've done," he replied painfully. "But there's no going back now."

He hurried to the upper floor and tapped twice on the Jaegers' door. Silence. He knocked again, and Hermann Jaeger opened the door.

"Afraid we missed you," McKenzie said with impressive nonchalance. "We had to leave the garden. Did you see what happened? We only caught the aftermath. We were held up along the U–Bahn line."

Jaeger showed vast disinterest, but he stepped aside to let us in. The room looked even more gloomy and unsettled than on our last visit. A couple of battered canvas bags and a black attaché case stood in a corner. The other novelty was a stained folding screen which blocked off the far side of the room. Wilhelm Jaeger was not in evidence.

His brother turned to me. "We were prevented from coming. What happened in the Englischergarten, Fräulein Peters?"

"An accident, I think. The gardens were full of police, and we saw an ambulance."

"It must have been a riding accident," Philip added. "Lots of horses around. Anyway, we realized it wasn't the right time and place for our meeting."

"We have nothing to fear from the West German police," Hermann said with soft insinuating menace. I thought that McKenzie must have been in an awful state to have considered a man so exceptionally ugly.

"It was all a bit too public," Philip replied. "And anyway, I don't like ambulances." He affected a fussy, slightly effeminate style which lent this a certain credibility.

"And where's your brother?"

Jaeger took my arm as though to emphasize the seriousness of the situation. "He was taken suddenly ill. He has — " he hesitated, seeking the English, "ulcers, bleeding ulcers."

"I'm sorry to hear that."

"I am getting ready to take him to the doctor. That was why we didn't meet you. I contacted your hotel, but there was no answer from your rooms."

"Perhaps we could settle our business first," McKenzie said. "The situation has changed slightly, Hermann. I think the three of us can now conclude the deal very rapidly."

"Things have changed a good deal, Herr Doktor," Jaeger agreed. He rocked slightly on the balls of his feet like an athlete.

"Where is your brother?" I repeated and walked around the screen before he could answer. Wilhelm was lying on the same battered couch he'd occupied during our previous visit. His skin matched its dingy cover, and the lines on his face had been deepened by pain. He did not move except to raise the gun he was holding.

"Stay back, Fräulein," he said in a hoarse, hesitant voice. "We are desperate men."

Hermann spoke rapidly in German. His brother nodded without lowering the pistol. Philip added something of his own, but the man on the couch remained frozen, like a grotesque Etruscan tomb statue.

"You can be of help," Hermann said to me. "My brother's condition is serious. He must have attention."

"You'll need to call an ambulance. He doesn't look fit to walk."

Jaeger showed his teeth. "My brother would be helpless in a hospital — at the mercy of anyone anxious to prevent the delivery of his scientific knowledge."

"He should ask for political asylum, Herr Jaeger. I believe refugees from East Germany are automatically given citizenship here."

"And in doing so he might be killed. I warned Herr Doktor in Frankfurt of the presence of East German agents. We will not trust government protection and hospital security." He spoke scornfully; perhaps he knew their limitations.

"Your brother certainly needs a doctor."

"But he needs one we can trust." He turned to McKenzie, "Did you come by car?"

"Yes. It's up the street."

"What make?"

"A Mercedes sedan."

"That will do. You will take us to Nuremberg. We have friends there who can treat Wilhelm. Get the car, Philip. Fräulein Peters will help me." He nodded to his brother, then added, "Perhaps we can settle our business there. We will see how it works out, Herr Doktor, once my brother is well." He spoke with complete confidence, even with a note of subtle condescension, which was extraordinary for a man in his position.

"Oh," Philip said. "All right. Nuremberg — there's nowhere nearer? I mean, for your brother's sake?" I think he understood then that the Jaegers might be playing a more ruthless game than he had anticipated.

Jaeger did not answer. When McKenzie left the apartment, Hermann pointed to the canvas bags. "You will carry those, please, Fräulein, and walk in front of us always. Slowly. Neither you nor Dr. McKenzie nor your company's money is essential to us now. Keep that in mind."

"But remember you need us to get to Nuremberg."

Jaeger just smiled. After a few moments, he asked, "Has Herr Doktor gotten the car yet?"

I went to the window. "He's parked in front of the doorway."

"Good. Come over here, Fräulein Peters. That's right. Now, don't move. Even in his present condition Wilhelm is an expert marksman." Hermann opened one of the canvas bags and removed a square leather case. Inside were some vials and a hypodermic needle. He rolled up his brother's sleeve, wiped off a square of skin and injected a clear fluid. The pistol Wilhelm held did not waver. Hermann put away the drug and took the weapon. He spoke in German, but I understood that he had administered a powerful painkiller. Then he helped his brother to his feet.

"Take the bags, Fräulein. I will carry the black case."

I opened the door, picked up their luggage and started downstairs. Hermann and Wilhelm struggled painfully behind. By the time McKenzie had helped Hermann get the sick man into the back seat, the older Jaeger seemed barely conscious.

"Is he all right?" McKenzie asked. Like me, he didn't fancy transporting even a phony scientist's corpse.

"I have given him some morphine," Hermann said. "He will manage the trip to Nuremberg."

McKenzie went to start the car.

"We will let Fräulein Peters drive," Jaeger said, "and you will sit in the front seat." He patted the bulge in his coat pocket, significantly. Then he climbed into the back beside his brother, and we turned onto Nymphenburgerstrasse and headed across town for the E6, the main route north. McKenzie gave me directions, while the Jaegers remained stolidly silent, Wilhelm asleep, Hermann watching every turn and every move with almost feral alertness. He was not a presence conducive to conversation, although in any case, neither McKenzie nor I had anything very clever to say. Until after we crossed the Danube, I occupied myself with maneuvering in the high-speed autobahn traffic and wondering how best to extract the papers from the Jaegers and ourselves from trouble. Probably McKenzie was thinking along similar lines, although that is not certain, because he looked glum and miserable. For his sake, I hoped he still believed Andy Ravelle was worth the effort.

"You will take the next exit from the autobahn, Fräulein."

That was unexpected. "Why?"

"My brother needs something to drink. We will take the next exit. I believe that will bring us out near Denkendorf — a short detour only."

In the rear mirror I could see Wilhelm's gray face; the glazed eyes were open.

"Is it safe for him to have something to drink?"

"Do not trouble yourself, Fräulein. Take the next exit." He put his hand lightly on McKenzie's shoulder. "Just remember that our friend the doctor is no longer necessary."

McKenzie stiffened and sat up straight in his seat. I did not think that Jaeger would attempt to eliminate Philip and me so soon — not unless his brother was either very much worse or very much better than he appeared; but as we left the main road and entered the forest, I grew less confident. This was the Altmuhl Valley: a large nature park occupied the south bank of the river and the dark woodland extended all the way to the point where the Altmuhl joins the Danube. It was a lonely area, and, depending on one's plans, as convenient for roads running east to the Czech border as north to Nuremberg. I glanced in the mirror, but Hermann's disagreeable terra-cotta mask told me nothing, except what I already knew: that he was both violent and unscrupulous.

"It's starting to rain again," McKenzie remarked. He had not spoken since the outskirts of Munich.

I switched on the wipers. The rain was light and misty, cloaking the forest in a soft velvety haze, whitish and mysterious, like a set for Swan Lake or Les Sylphides. In the current production, Jaeger was obviously the evil magician: whatever he summoned up from the mist would surely be unpleasant.

"There is a turnoff about a mile ahead. We will stop there."

A few houses appeared along the road, the outskirts of some small village. What lay beyond, at Jaeger's turnoff, we never learned, because around the next bend was a roadblock. Two green-and-white patrol cars were parked at the sides of the road, and a trooper stood in the middle to flag down passing cars. Wilhelm saw them, too, and gave a groan which resolved itself into an unintelligible German expression.

"Good God!" Philip exclaimed. He went dead white.

"No reason to think it's for us," I said quickly, a conviction almost immediately undermined by guilty conscience.

"That is right," Hermann said, as I slowed the car. "You will be very careful, both of you."

The policeman waved me to the side. I stopped and rolled down the window. He stepped to the car, glancing rapidly at its occupants.

"*Guten Tag.*"

"*Guten Tag, Herr Schutzmann.*"

"*Amerikanisch?*"

"Ja. Doktor McKenzie hier sprechen Deutsch."

"Gut." He asked for my license and examined the papers for the Mercedes, while his colleague made a minute inspection of the front and side of our car. In the rear mirror, I could see Hermann staring casually out into the rain. His brother, with what must have been a considerable effort of will, had drawn himself almost upright in the seat. I wondered what his injury really was and whether or not it had occurred in the Englischergarten. The officer returned.

"He says we can go now," McKenzie relayed; then we were waved onto the road.

"Ist ein Lebensmittelladen in der Nähe?"

The patrolman pointed up the road. *"Nur ein wenig Entfernung. Links."*

"Tell him we will return through in a few minutes, Philip."

This was relayed, and the policeman smiled and nodded. Two minutes farther on, I stopped at a small grocery store. Hermann was not pleased, but he accompanied McKenzie in to buy some mineral water, while his brother kept the revolver pressed against the back of my neck. I told myself that for a while, at least, we were out of danger. Hermann's plans for removing us had just been postponed, because the police would surely remember the car and the number of its passengers.

"What was that all about anyway?" I asked when they returned.

McKenzie handed in a bottle of water, then shut his door. "Hit-and-run driver farther down the line. That's why they checked the front end."

Hermann gave his brother some of the water, which he drank gratefully. At the roadblock, we were waved straight through, and Wilhelm slumped back on the seat with a soft moan; his momentary revival had taken a good deal out of him.

"To Nuremberg, Herr Jaeger?"

"As fast as possible." Perhaps he had misjudged his brother's condition.

I must have seemed too relieved, because Hermann leaned over the front seat, his arm across McKenzie's shoulder.

"Herr McKenzie is very clever," he said.

"He is our best chemist."

Jaeger laughed. "Yes, but he is clever in other ways, too. We are taking my brother to a specialist in Nuremburg. An old friend of the family. You were quite convincing, Philip. I think we'll keep you." He drew the words out softly, taking an almost sadistic pleasure in teasing McKenzie. I stepped on the gas in irritation, sending the powerful car roaring down the empty road toward the autobahn. Wilhelm groaned, his eyes closed, and Hermann was thrown back against the seat. He glanced at his brother, decided he was all right, then sat forward again.

"Fräulein Peters likes you, Philip," he said, looking at me with undisguised distaste. "Does she know all your talents?"

"Careful," I said, more to McKenzie than to Jaeger.

Philip's look of misery increased, but he did not answer.

Jaeger laughed gently. Our situation gave him a sense of power as compensation for whatever the police roadblock had prevented. He was a man who might well go too far in satisfying his impulse to dominate. "In my situation, a man cannot be too careful. But Philip, now, is not careful. Has he confided in you? I think so. That was not careful." He shook his head. "He ought to have trusted me more — or less. He has trusted me just the wrong amount." And he patted McKenzie's shoulder again.

There was a sound from the back seat. The rear mirror showed nothing amiss except that Wilhelm seemed to have passed out again.

"Sit around, Herr Doktor," Jaeger ordered sharply. "He has just dropped the bottle of water."

"Is he all right for God's sake?" McKenzie asked.

Hermann checked his brother's pulse. "*Ja,* but he is quite weak. You must drive to the limit, Fräulein."

The rain had intensified, leaving the autobahn slick with water which the passing cars churned into great sheets of spray. "The road isn't good."

"That is your problem."

"How far out are we?"

"Less than an hour."

The light faded, and the wipers carved wet gray tunnels from the downpour. The open window sucked in mild, dank air that mingled with the smoke from McKenzie's chain of cigarettes. As we approached Nuremberg, the traffic increased; and by the time the city was in sight, I had to keep all my attention on the road. Soon we reached the tower marking the start of the thick, black fortifications. It rose, massive and uncompromising, out of the gloom, German and Nuremberg flags thrust from its upper story like crusaders' pennons. I stopped for a traffic light next to the bahnhof. "Where to?" I asked.

Jaeger didn't answer. I had not noticed what was happening behind me.

"Which way?" I repeated as a truck raced its motor impatiently behind us.

Philip turned at this, started to say something, then, "Jesus! What's happened?"

There was disaster in his voice. I jockeyed the car through the traffic and stopped at the first available stretch of curb. Wilhelm was lying in the back seat, a dribble of blood running from his nose. Hermann had ripped open his jacket and shirt, both of which were darkly stained, to reveal a thick, blood-soaked bandage across his ribs. Hermann was covering this with a piece of toweling, but it was obvious that Dr. Jaeger had been bleeding heavily.

"*Gehen Sie! Gehen Sie!*"

There were crowds of people milling about the sidewalk waiting for buses and walklights. I slid the car into gear. "Which way? He needs help right now."

"This way. Toward Erlenstegen."

I caught a glimpse of his wet red hands. Wilhelm moaned softly.

"Erlenstegen?"

"*Ja, ja.* Toward the northeast."

"Can't you give him another shot?" McKenzie asked. Wilhelm's breathing sounded hoarse and uncertain. If he died in the car, we'd all be in a fix.

"Too weak. Do not turn around, Philip. I am still armed."

"I didn't mean," McKenzie began, surprised. "No! Turn up here."

I wrenched the wheel. "This street?"

"No, dammit! The main road! Follow the trams."

I squeezed the Mercedes recklessly between a bus and a Volkswagen and made the turn.

"*Vorsicht!*" Jaeger yelled.

"Shut up and let me drive!" I slammed on the brakes at the next light and looked back. Hermann seemed to have gotten things somewhat under control. "How far?"

"Ten — fifteen minutes at the most — if you don't wreck the car."

"You'd have more to explain than I would. What happened to him?"

"He met an old enemy."

That was a possibility.

"Stay on this street?"

"Yes, all the way out."

We passed a park and left the walled medieval town behind. The modern concrete block buildings of the rebuilt city gave way to red brick apartments and then to substantial older homes, some set handsomely behind fenced lawns with big shade trees. Just beyond the roundabout that marked the limits of a tram line, Jaeger directed us under a railroad bridge and then off to a steep side road. Thick woods of beech and fir rose on one side; on the other was a wide strip of meadowland where silvery clumps of willows floated in the mist. There were several large brick houses along this grassland; Jaeger directed us to the last of these, a three-story building set well away from the rest and separated from both its neighbors and the street by hedges and trees. The drive ran through a weedy garden to a gravel patch behind the house. A German shepherd stepped curiously toward the car as we stopped, and out the back door came a tall, robust man in a blue work shirt holding a black umbrella against the drizzle. He reminded me of Jürgen Honiss. Who had rented our car? His wife's brother? An employee's cousin? Too bad. There were going to be some telltale stains on the upholstery.

Chapter 10

THE MAN WITH THE UMBRELLA opened my door and motioned me out. He had restless brown eyes and flat cheekbones that slanted away from a thin hawk-like nose to hide in curly light brown hair and sideburns. He addressed Hermann in incomprehensible gutturals before shouting toward the house. An old woman, bent double like a fat German sausage, appeared in the doorway, then disappeared again like a clockwork figure. In her place, a slight man of indeterminate age and brisk, almost military, bearing emerged. He smoothed back his thin black hair and began snapping orders to the man with the umbrella, to the dog, to Hermann, and to Philip. This was the doctor, and he jerked open the rear door of the Mercedes and took a quick look at Wilhelm.

"Tragen Sie ihn zu dem Haus," he commanded. He stepped aside, shaking his head angrily, and wiped his hands on a handkerchief. McKenzie and Hermann lifted the injured man from the car and, under the shelter of the umbrella, carried him toward the house. The doctor and I followed. There was a struggle to get the groaning patient safely up the steps and through the narrow doorway, and the men were dripping with rain and sweat before this maneuver was accomplished. The old woman yelled at the dog to stay out, then the doctor led the way from the kitchen to a hall and through sliding oak doors at the back of the living room. They laid the injured man on the dining-room table.

The functionary with the umbrella folded his implement and gestured toward a chair covered in threadbare tapestry. *"Bleiben Sie hier, Fräulein,"* he ordered before he left to engage the woman in a loud and probably long-running argument. I scarcely had time to examine the foyer, a dark oak-paneled affair fronting an even darker and more ornate stairway, when McKenzie reappeared, looking severely shaken.

"They need hot water," he said.

"Ask in the kitchen."

He interrupted the squabble; a rattling of pots and a running of water followed. Then the guard brought in our luggage, and the woman, very gray, very bent, and very heavy, shuffled after him. Motioning for us to follow, she began an assault on the stair, dragging her swollen legs up one step at a time and wheezing like a tea kettle. She had the same toast-colored eyes as the bodyguard, but lacked his uneasy watchfulness. Age, distilling her personality, had eliminated both uncertainty and variety. When she turned to look at us on the landing, her eyes held only a settled malevolence.

The rooms on the second floor fronted a hall which circled the stairwell. At one end of this passage, the resident crone stopped and pointed to a heavy door. Behind this, we found a small sitting room with a fireplace, flanked by two bedrooms. The large windows in the main room looked out over the fields.

"She says we're to stay here for now. Herr Jaeger will be up shortly," Philip reported.

The woman shut the door with a disgruntled bang and snapped the lock. I put down my bag and walked around. The rooms were square, of fair size, and potentially elegant, although the paint and wallpaper were frowzy with age and neglect. The furniture consisted of large, ill-matched pieces of prewar vintage.

"I suppose they rented this as is."

McKenzie shrugged. The Jaegers' living arrangements were a minor concern.

"I'm filthy," he said, surveying shirt and hands stained and spotted with Wilhelm's blood.

"Is he going to make it?"

"I didn't see the actual wound. It may be only superficial, but he's lost a lot of blood. He'll surely need a transfusion."

"Perhaps his brother's the same type — if they really are brothers."

This was another area McKenzie declined to explore, preferring to set about removing the traces of our gory afternoon. While he washed, I examined the main room, looking behind the drapes and along the baseboard. Nothing. Ditto behind the only picture, a cheap lithograph of a little girl in pantaloons and sunbonnet, cuddling a smug rabbit. One of the windows opened onto a shallow balcony, and I stepped outside. The rain had slacked off again to mere mist, a soft damp blanket that turned the meadows into a Chinese painting and added a suitably gothic touch to the thick stands of conifers beyond. Below on the brick-and-cobblestone patio, the large shepherd paced restlessly, with an alertness that reminded me of Herr Jaeger.

"Come out here a minute."

"Aren't we wet enough already?" McKenzie grumbled. He looked emotionally exhausted. I didn't feel too chipper myself, but he had certainly gotten the worst of it. I wondered how much of his surprising will power remained intact.

"Does Hermann still have the papers with him?"

"Yes, and he'll keep them under lock and key."

"Could you rewrite them from memory?"

"Could, but they'd still have the process. They would just sell it to another company."

"New World would have it first — for less."

McKenzie shook his head stubbornly. "I want my money."

"We could work something out. In cash."

"Huh. It's all academic anyway. They've got us here, and they'll probably keep us here." He leaned over the rail. The dog looked up and began a little dance of excitement. "Look at that brute. *It* would raise hell if no one else noticed our exit."

"You worry about the wrong things. First decide what to do, then worry about how to do it."

"The scientific method precisely. But I know what to do: make the deal. We can carry through with the Jaegers, because they've had some unforeseen problems, too. They'll want to get their money and bug out of here as soon as Wilhelm can be moved."

"But remember, Philip, that I control the money. You may be

willing to take chances; I'm inclined to be a little more conserva-
tive. They don't get a dime until we're out of here. Period. Any
other plan and we risk winding up like the guy in the English Garden."

"Ah, *der Englischergarten*." As we turned a shadow moved
behind the curtain, and Hermann Jaeger opened the window.

"Come in, come in out of the rain. We will talk about the *Englischergarten*. Americans are so privileged, so fortunate — "
he paused, looking at McKenzie, "so innocent."

There was something to that from his point of view.

"We will let you make the explanations, then," I said. "How
is Wilhelm?"

Hermann finished rolling down his sleeves before he answered. "He needed blood. Otherwise, the doctor says he will
be all right."

"No internal injuries?"

"He hopes not."

"Good. He can be moved fairly soon. Perhaps he would be
wise to follow our original plan and come to the States."

Herr Jaeger did not answer this immediately but sat down in a
ponderous silence. He did not intend to let the initiative slip to
our side. "I think we should delay that, Fräulein Peters."

"As you like. Of course we are still interested in the patent,
but Dr. McKenzie and I have other work to do. You could get in
touch with us when your brother is able to travel."

Jaeger smiled slightly, anticipating the announcement that
McKenzie and I would have to postpone our departure. "Herr
Doktor said that the situation had changed, Fräulein. He was
correct. My brother's injury has complicated all our plans."

McKenzie had not spoken during this time. Suddenly he
asked, "Who was the man you killed?"

"What man, Philip?"

"The man in the garden."

"You said earlier it was a riding accident."

"We don't have time for this," I interrupted. Jaeger could
play cat and mouse with McKenzie another day. "Whether you
decide to come to the States or not, you and your brother are

going to have to leave here. I don't see that you can risk contacting other oil firms and offering the patent openly. We want it and we are prepared to pay for it, but only after Dr. McKenzie and I have left here. We don't make any arrangements while we are here."

"You have no need to be alarmed, Fräulein. I don't see why you take that tone," Jaeger said with a resentful severity that I found reassuring: he wasn't ready to come out into the open quite yet. "The man in the garden was an East German agent, who had kept me under surveillance for quite some time. I believed, wrongly, that I had lost him on the way to Munich." He folded his arms and sniffed. "One reason that we needed a great deal more money than you expected was to avoid such people. This house for example. No doubt he picked up your trail. You two are fairly obvious targets. If you should leave, it would be a simple matter, wouldn't it, for them either to pick you up and ask you where we are or to wait and follow you once we made contact again. My brother will be helpless for a day or two, so we can't allow that."

"None of that need arise — if we fly directly back to the States."

Jaeger shook his head. "You might decide our agreement is not worth keeping. You do not have the investment in this matter that my brother and I do."

"Herr Jaeger, the money we promised will not be transferred while we are still in this house. Even if we agreed on the plan, the company would be extremely suspicious."

Jaeger looked at McKenzie.

"There's no advantage for Philip in that deal, either," I said sharply. I liked McKenzie but I hadn't decided yet how much I could rely on him.

"Philip has trusted me so far, haven't you, Philip?" Jaeger spoke softly, but he got a response.

"Don't threaten us," McKenzie said, turning to face him. "You're not as independent of me as you think."

Jaeger's expression turned nasty. "What do you mean?"

"We will discuss it with Wilhelm, as soon as he's able. Then

Anna and I will settle on a cash deal. She's agreed to that already, so I'll still get my share."

Jaeger stepped toward him, grabbing for his arm, but McKenzie pulled away and walked toward the window. "Don't try to do without us, that's all. You'd be making a very big mistake." That conveyed something to Jaeger, if not to me. He whirled around and left the room, slamming the door. McKenzie's control evaporated. He sat down hastily in one of the chairs and put his head in his hands. "God, what a fool I've been!" he said.

"You've made an impression on Herr Jaeger, though."

"He's threatened to kill me — in so many words."

"No doubt he's considering it. Minus us, he'd have a free hand — if he can wait to play it. Fortunately, I don't think he can risk any more bodies at the moment, especially bodies that New World is watching over."

"He can be very violent," McKenzie continued in a reminiscent whisper. "And that man in the park — "

That had been flamboyantly violent, all right. "I can't say I approve your taste."

"I've got some insurance," he said, ignoring this remark. "Come here." He leaned forward, and I knelt down beside his chair. McKenzie whispered very softly in my ear: "There are some pieces missing."

I sat back on my heels and stared at thim. McKenzie nodded.

"And they don't know?"

"Not yet. It's a complex document. Wilhelm will see sooner or later. I rather thought sooner, but no doubt he's had a lot on his mind."

"No doubt." That opened up new possibilities. "In some ways, this puts us in *more* danger rather than less."

"Yes, but to pull it off, they need us both healthy. We can gamble for a day or two." McKenzie slouched in the chair and a little color returned to his face. "I think we can do it," he said. "I really think we can," and he gave a faint smile.

I knew his mercurial temperament well enough not to argue. McKenzie held aces all right, but they might not win in current company. Perhaps that was in itself the attraction: thugs fascinated him. Or danger. Or both. Andy Ravelle had presented the potential for disaster, but even he could hardly top a night in Nuremberg with a murderer, a man bled half to death, a crew of cutthroats, and a scientific patent worth millions. That was glamor. That was casting off dull care and laboratory routine and emotional sacrifice and whatever else McKenzie's narrow life had formerly encompassed. Mundane affairs were discarded with a vengeance — and for high stakes. My own passion for gambling had, unfortunately, atrophied over the years. I sat down opposite McKenzie and put my feet up. I felt like staying there and vegetating; at the moment, I did not share his taste for melodramatic excitement at all.

Chapter 11

AFTER DINNER, McKenzie and Jaeger began to play chess, watched by the doctor, who sat smoking his pipe between visits to his patient. The two formidable domestics adjourned to the kitchen, and I lay with my feet up on the window seat, admiring the stills in a German film magazine. I did not want to leave McKenzie to talk with Jaeger alone, for there was a reckless streak in him and his hints had already unsettled our host. I observed them over the chessboard. Philip, obviously a good player, sprawled, relaxed, one arm dangling loosely over the back of his chair. He tapped the ash off his cigarette, glanced at the board, and then resumed his contemplation of the handsome coffered ceiling. He evidently had his opponent in a bad spot, because Jaeger sat hunched forward, tapping his knuckles lightly against his teeth. Now and again, they spoke in German, their conversation proceeding in bits and snatches that left me uncertain whether their subject was the game or some larger stake. Perhaps the latter, because McKenzie's nonchalance held suppressed excitement, and Jaeger, crouched over his pawns and bishops, seemed ready to pounce.

At eleven, the doctor announced that Wilhelm was awake and apparently out of danger. His brother relaxed noticeably, and, at this point, the evening broke up, and McKenzie and I said good night.

"What did Jaeger have to say?" I asked when we reached the landing.

"Nothing much," McKenzie yawned. "I'm exhausted, aren't you?"

"You played chess long enough."

"How domestic you sound!" he said archly. "I wanted to beat him when I had the chance."

"Has he figured it out?"

"He's aware of the situation, but he can't be sure I'm not bluffing until he talks to Wilhelm. Well, good night," Philip concluded and disappeared quickly behind his door. Resigned to sleeplessness, I went to my room and lay on top of the bed, intending to remain awake until I learned what was going on. Far away in the quiet night a dog barked and a train passed over the tracks on the bridge with a gentle rumble. A faint scent of wurst and cabbage lingered in the air. When I looked at my watch again, it was after four.

"Damn!" I sat up, fully awake. There was not a sound. I left my room cautiously. Across the sitting room, Philip's door stood half open, and closer inspection showed his empty bed. "Damn, damn, damn!" I was prepared to charge downstairs and confront the pair of them, when I found the door of the suite was locked. I rattled the handle. No luck. I kicked the door and hollered. No answer. My first impulse was to go to the window, denounce both McKenzie and Jaeger, and arouse the whole neighborhood. Reflection revealed the folly of that procedure. I listened at the door until I was convinced that no one was stirring. Then I went out onto the balcony.

The house was set on a slope which fell away rapidly, giving the building two stories with a gabled attic in the front, closer to three in the rear, where the basement was practically all above ground. This, combined with the high ceilings in the rooms, meant that the balcony was a long way above the paved court — too far to drop without risking a broken leg or ankle. I pushed aside the curtains and noticed the substantial cords they ran on. These might do. If I could lower myself even part way, reaching the ground safely would be a better bet. Cutting half a dozen lengths of sashcord, I tested each by slinging it over the top of the bedroom door and trying if it would bear my weight. The first was rotten and snapped, sending me abruptly to the floor. The rest, fortunately, were relatively new and tied together formed a decent rope. Next, I emptied my wallet, stuffed the marks I was carrying in my back pocket and put my passport in my windbreaker in case I decided to make my exit permanent.

Then I examined the balcony, selected what appeared to be a stout post, fastened the rope and, before fear of heights could intervene, crossed the rail and prepared to descend.

The dog growled. Not loudly; it was a real pro. Just a soft, even, gentle, growl. I looked down, causing the rope to spin and swing a little away from the balcony. The kennel, until then out of sight, was directly beneath. The shepherd slept with its head and forepaws extending from the door and the large velvet ears and pointed black muzzle were now turned alertly in my direction. It swung its head like a small, sensitive radar dish, decided I was suspicious, and came out to investigate. Then it growled again and began pacing back and forth like a conscientious, but not particularly bright, watchman, uncertain whether or not to raise the alarm. I whispered down in both English and German that it was an excellent dog, a prince of beasts, but either it was a worldly wise brute or my pronunciation failed, because it was not mollified. I climbed up the rope and scrambled back over the rail of the balcony. Reassured, the animal sat down, its eyes trained in my direction.

To be outwitted by McKenzie and Jaeger was one thing; to be thwarted by their fuzzy mascot was another, and the gable roof, which sloped steeply down on either side, suggested another approach. I could not reach the roof from the balcony or from the top of the protective railing, but it was still temptingly close. I found a chair which raised me level with the rail. A little more height and I could make it. There followed frantic efforts to persuade a square table to pass the narrow rectangular window. When it was firmly wedged between the house and the railing, I balanced the chair on top, slung the coil of rope over my shoulder, and started up. There was a dicey moment when I had to lean out over empty space to reach the roof, and another, when, having committed myself, I had to trust to the firmness and resolve of one particular red tile. It held, and braced against the sides of the corrugated orange valley formed by the two sections of the roof, I recovered my breath.

Over the tops of the trees shielding the house, I could see the traintracks and, beyond them, the start of the black and substantial forest. The dog was out of sight, hidden in the shadows of the eaves, and I found it safer not to look down at the hard wet cobblestones. When I could postpone no longer, I turned to the main business of the evening. The rain had left the tiles slippery, and, on my upward progress, I touched several which slithered away from foot or hand, sending my heart into high and emptying my lungs with a gasp. At the top was a view of the dark Nuremberg meadows: damp, bucolic, historic, and all too far below my miserable perch astride the crown of the roof. I edged toward a chimney and clasped it in relief. As I had anticipated, this side of the house was constructed like the other, with a short, projecting gable which probably held a suite of rooms similar to the one McKenzie and I occupied. With luck, there would be a balcony. If not, my imagination balked; I was already too old for these alpine endeavors, and the current escapade was accelerating senescence.

The improvised rope was fairly short, and much of its length had to be sacrificed in anchoring it securely about the chimney. If there was no balcony or if the distance was too great, I would have to scramble back to attempt the front of the building and the porch roof. Delaying the precipitous descent, I tugged at the cord, tightening the slipknot to test it once more. I reminded the coward within that while it would be ridiculous to break my neck climbing down, it would be even more ridiculous to be discovered shivering behind the chimney pots come sunrise. Finally, focusing on a patch of tile, I turned around and lowered myself, hand over hand, until one foot reached out into space. Then I knelt on the roof and looked over the edge. I was only a few feet above a large multiple window, and although there was an unbroken drop to the drive below, there'd be enough rope to take me as far as the sill. Two of the windows were open, and it looked tricky, but not impossible, to re-enter the house that way. I listened for a few moments, but everything remained quiet, and the weedy garden told me nothing to the contrary. Having decided, it was best not to hesitate. I lay on the roof and, inch by inch, squirmed my way over the edge. I rested on my forearms for an instant, then trusted to the sashcord and released the tiles, scraping my elbow and alarming my stomach as I swung free into space. I had misjudged the distance.

Gently, I swayed back and forth, and the tiles above made a crunching sound as they chewed on the rope like squirrels. I did not think I was strong enough to pull myself back up, because the muscles in my arms were already beginning to quiver. I was committed to the window, and, mobilizing my will power, I released one hand, slowly moving it down the cord. There was a bit of rope left, and I edged lower until, dangling with both hands at the very end, I was within reach of the casement. The windows opened out, and I could touch one fragile-looking sash. I didn't fancy having it give way if I relied on it, so I began trying to open the window farther, although this involved swinging on the rope and increasing its chances of fraying. The tiles shifted slightly overhead, and, as the sash swung open, I banged into the rough brick wall with a jolt. I squinted up at the rope wedged between the edges of two tiles. Then I tested the sash with one hand, and pushed away and swung sideways to gain momentum. There was a sharper crack from above, but one foot touched the sill, and, throwing all my weight forward, I snatched at the casement. I struck my nose on the top of the window and my feet slipped off the sill, but when the rope fell slackly over my shoulder and followed the broken tile to the ground, I remained, clinging by my fingertips. A lace curtain, disturbed by the night air, blew across my face like a ghost, and I dropped unsteadily onto the sill, then climbed down into the dark room.

There was the sound of someone breathing. I froze behind the curtain, but when no one challenged me, I pushed aside the drape to find a bed only a few feet away. An I–V bottle was rigged on a stand, and, beside it, Wilhelm lay asleep, a blanket pulled up under his chin. He was probably still under sedation. I closed the window, then, after listening at his door for a few seconds, stepped out cautiously. It had taken a good deal of effort to get across that ornate stairwell.

The lights had been left burning in the upstairs hall, and they engendered little red and green goblins' eyes after the predawn grayness outside. As I adjusted to their light, I heard voices:

McKenzie's, Jaeger's — one or two others. The sound seemed that of a conference becoming a quarrel, but then even at best there's a certain abrasiveness to German. The foyer below was empty, and the kitchen, too, was deserted; but off this room was a storage pantry, unnoticed during the events of the afternoon. There I discovered a door ajar, and when I eased it open, worn stone steps leading down to the cellar and to what was now an open altercation. Jaeger had clearly abandoned all pretense at subtlety and was roaring abuse at McKenzie. Although their German was far beyond my comprehension, it was clear that he was nearly out of control and that McKenzie, for his part, was holding his ground with an almost hysterical persistence. I crouched on the step to see. Light came from a room in the right side of the basement. With the noise they were making, there was little chance of their noticing my descent into the shadows and cobwebs behind the bottom steps. In the room ahead were a hanging lamp and a couple of straight wooden chairs. Philip was sitting tensely in one, while Jaeger, standing with one foot on the other, advanced what sounded like a final offer. Behind Philip and a little to one side stood the bodyguard, his arms folded, the lamplight casting a mask of shadow under his eyes like a lineman's blacking.

It was an ominous grouping, a Grosz or a Beckmann come to life, but strikingly logical. It was the predictable outcome of the relationship between McKenzie and Jaeger, an emotional calculus that could end only in violence, a violence, perhaps, that had been inevitable from the beginning. I shivered, and apprehension awakened all the bumps and scrapes I'd acquired on my scramble over the roof. The cellar was cold, yet I found myself sweating from fear and exertion, as I tried to get my bearings. On the other side of the stair was what appeared to be a door to the outside, and, behind me, the dark maw of a half empty coalbin. Underfoot in the dust were a couple of bricks and a short length of firewood, which I grabbed as a weapon against Jaeger and his henchman.

"You won't figure it out — not without my help," McKenzie said.

"There is no more time to play with you. Give me the rest or neither you nor Fräulein Peters will leave here."

"I want the money," McKenzie said stubbornly. "Let us go, and I guarantee she'll get it. New World wants that patent, and they won't ask where it came from. Same with your brother. Ship him to the States and the two of you will be on easy street."

The guard interrupted, protesting the use of English, and Jaeger responded to them both in furious German. McKenzie jumped up, but Jaeger struck him heavily in the face, knocking him back into the chair, which almost tipped over. Although scarcely athletic, McKenzie was not without resources, and alone he might have made a fair showing even against Jaeger. Hermann was not bound, however, by the restraints of fair play. McKenzie bounced up, threw a punch that Jaeger dodged, and then, after a brutally brief scuffle, was pinioned by the bodyguard. Perhaps there was a point when I might have intervened and tipped the balance, but it vanished in an instant. Before I could reach the room, McKenzie was helpless, and Jaeger, armed or not, was more than a match for me.

Hermann spoke. McKenzie shook his head, and Jaeger struck him in the solar plexus. McKenzie collapsed forward, gasping, his glasses shattering on the stones; and Jaeger ran his short, stubby fingers gently over his knuckles, his lips drawn into a tight, straight line. Sadistic bastard. I clenched the stick of firewood until the splinters dug into my palm. Jaeger spoke again, his voice softer, almost a whisper, full of secrets, and I heard the sound of another punch, as I turned away, sick inside. McKenzie retched, but refused to give in. There was a welter of blows, the pulpy sound of bone striking flesh, then the light swung, and I saw the black box hanging on the wall just a few feet from the door. As Jaeger and his henchman talked above McKenzie's groans, I caught my breath, slid along the wall, and tugged the box open with a snap. There was a sudden silence from the other room, and I dropped the wood and began pulling fuses out of their sockets. One, two, three — nothing, just a nightmarish silence and brightness. Four, five — the bodyguard's hoarse warning, Jaeger's approach. Six — everything went black. I kicked the fuses aside, grabbed the stick of firewood and slashed at the figure before me. He grabbed my shoulder, and I swung again, causing a cry of rage and surprise. Jaeger fell backwards, colliding with his partner.

"Philip! This way!" I yelled.

There was a confused struggle. Jaeger exclaimed *"Sicherung"* and groped his way toward the fuse box.

"Anna, where are you?"

The bodyguard grabbed my hair. I tried to fight away from him, couldn't, heard Jaeger rattling about with the fuses, Philip stumbling through the doorway, and then the sound of footsteps above. The pantry door banged open, casting a pale light over our disorderly tableau. I struck hard and low at the bodyguard and leaped desperately toward freedom.

The doctor's voice cut through the confusion: *"Die Polizei! die Polizei!"* he shouted.

Chapter 12

WE FROZE IN THE HALF LIGHT like children playing Giant Steps: Jaeger still gripping the fusebox, McKenzie leaning against the doorway, the bodyguard and I poised near the stair. Then Jaeger dropped the fuses, shoved past me, and mounted the steps two at a time. There were men on the front porch, and one of them was working on the lock. At this, the guard abandoned us and wrenched open the cellar door. His feet crunched over the gravel until stopped by a short, popping sound, like a champagne cork, followed by the thud of a heavy body striking the earth. McKenzie and I took refuge in the coalbin and waited. After a moment, we heard steps directly overhead.

Four men, I guessed, and I wondered exactly what sort of *Polizei* they were: *Bundesrepublik* cops investigating the murder case, East German counterespionage men after the Jaegers, or some even more exotic and less expected species? McKenzie drew in his breath sharply and pressed my arm. Someone crossed the gravel outside, then the dark silhouette of a man armed with an automatic weapon appeared in the opalescent light of the doorway. Entering the cellar, he switched on a flashlight and swept it over the stair, across the coalbin, down on the floor under the fuse box, into the room with the chairs and the now extinguished hanging light. We cowered against the wall and awaited our inevitable discovery.

The intruder lowered his weapon slightly and circled the steps, his light roving the walls of the room beyond like a giant creeping eye. Make a run for it — or stay? I glanced at McKenzie, who stood with his eyes closed, sweat pouring off his forehead. I didn't like the look of him. The cyclops returned, a round, bright blob about to engulf us. It flickered over our heads, began its descent, was distracted by footsteps on the stair.

"Richard?"

"Ja."

A second man appeared, and they held a hushed consultation before hurrying above. McKenzie and I breathed again; it sounded as if they were heading for the second floor. Then silence. The walls and floors were thick and the invading party too obviously disciplined for idle clatter. Motioning McKenzie to stay put, I checked our escape route. The morning sky had turned from gray to white, and bands of fog filled the gaps between the trees. The Mercedes was gone, the parking space empty except for the bodyguard who lay just at the edge of the gravel, discoloring the white pebbles with a thick, dark rivulet of blood. Over all hung a murky cotton-woolly atmosphere like the studio fog banks in old World War I movies and quite as fit to conceal an army. Uncertain whether the truncated form at the end of the lawn was a tree stump or a sentinel, I turned back, ready to recommend patience, as a nervous rattle of shots broke out above us. For an instant we hesitated in the doorway; when nothing moved, I seized McKenzie's arm and broke across the gravel and the short damp grass to the weeds and shrubbery dividing the yard from the fields and thickets beyond. We had only gone a few yards when we stumbled over the dog, sprawled in high grass. It was still breathing, and there was no sign of a wound. McKenzie bent down painfully and ruffled the animal's fur, revealing a short dart.

"Tranquilizer gun."

"Well prepared, whoever they are."

Philip showed no sign of moving, so I took his arm again and led him farther into the brush. It was too bad that the grass was so wet, for looking back, I could see our trail clearly. Unless the sun rose with an unprecedented burst of radiant heat — or the *Polizei* delayed reconnoitering the yard — we were going to be easy quarry. McKenzie gave a soft cough. He was holding his side in pain, and he was extrememly pale. When we reached the shelter of some yews and stopped to rest, he sat down on a log.

"How're you doing?"

"I think he broke a couple of ribs. Nothing too bad. Hurts like hell though."

It was obviously painful for him to speak. McKenzie held his wrist with two fingers.

"How's your pulse?"

"Going like a flamenco dancer."

"If that outfit's West German, we'd be smart to get some help."

"What if they're East German?"

"Could you tell — from their speech — from anything Jaeger said?"

"I wasn't really in shape to notice." He wiped his face on the back of his arm. "I can't see far — what's going on?"

I peered through the screen of branches at a couple of black cars parked in the front of the house. The shots had not been followed up. Either Jaeger had been shot or the attack force had been temporarily halted. One seemed as likely as the other.

"Nothing that I can see. Did Jaeger expect this sort of thing?" Was he prepared?"

Before Philip could answer there was an explosion, then another and the sound of renewed firing.

"Grenades," he said.

The window in what had been our rooms shattered. We could hear shouts, and suddenly there were a great many people in evidence. A car screeched around to the back of the building, and then men, armed and dressed in dark sweaters and raincoats, began to fan out over the lawn and across the fence to the meadows. Three headed in our direction. It was just a matter of time.

McKenzie stood up.

"What do you say?"

"I think I can make it as far as the road." He pointed to the nearby street which was pretty well screened by bushes and long grass.

"O.K. Then what? I don't see you getting much farther."

"There are trolleys, buses — we can stay undercover until the morning traffic starts."

That would have been my plan, too. "All right. Let's go, but if you get too weak, we'll have to give up."

"I'm all right, I'm all right," he replied, half embarrassed, and we started through the underbrush, McKenzie moving slowly, his head hanging. After a dozen yards or so, he put one arm around my shoulders. That seemed more painful but produced better progress. Behind us, the gunmen had circled the house, and several were clustered by the garage, talking. Another car pulled up, and a party of men scrambled over the fence behind the yard and headed for the stream.

"Maybe Jaeger or the doctor got away," I said. "If they chase him, we'll have a chance."

McKenzie wheezed along the rutted path for a few more minutes. "They'll find our luggage," he said.

"And your passport?"

"Yes."

"From that point of view, it would be better if they turn out to be East Germans. They're less liable to follow up on you."

McKenzie stopped, gasping. "I have to rest. Damn ribs are killing me."

"Let's get across the road, first."

He shook his head. "Can't walk and talk. Something I better tell you: Jaeger said last night he wasn't going to the States. That's just since the Englischergarten."

That struck an off chord all right. "He's scared of extradition, probably. The West Germans must have something on him or else he lied about the identity of the man in the garden. We can't worry about it now. We've got to get across here before they pick up our tracks."

We moved to the edge of the pavement. There was a short, but fairly steep, slope up to the main roadway, then another rise, covered with trees and vines before the railroad tracks and a squat concrete shelter.

"That's a station — you can flag locals from there," McKenzie whispered.

Down the street in one direction lay open meadows and what appeared to be pipes and equipment for a water works. Between us and town was the driveway into the Jaegers'. A truck blocked the entrance, and two men stood lounging against it.

"Can you make the main roadway?"

McKenzie looked at the rough and overgrown slope and hesitated.

"Once we get up there, we can pass the guards and head into Nuremberg. I'll find a car."

He nodded.

"Wait until they turn the other way. If we can get by them and into the suburbs, we'll have a few hours at least before they can do anything with your passport photo."

McKenzie looked even paler than before. He was in a lot of pain, of course, but I had an awful feeling that there might be more wrong with him than just emotional shock and smashed ribs.

"I'm O.K.," he whispered irritably, as if reading my thoughts.

I glanced back at the men on the truck. One had lit a cigarette, the other was walking in the direction of the house.

"Now."

We stepped into the street and the sudden panic of exposure. McKenzie's hard shoes rang on the asphalt, and he had to put his hand over his mouth to stifle a cough, but as we reached the grass, I saw that the Jaegers' yard was still quiet. The man at the truck had his back to us and was fiddling with the antenna of a walkie-talkie. We were going to make it after all. Then McKenzie stumbled and gasped. I caught him, but he remained bent over, supporting himself against the slope with one hand.

"What is it?"

"Just the pain. Maybe a lung."

He started to retch.

"We can't stay here. We're in plain sight. Either we give ourselves up or we get to the main road. Letting them catch us is the worst of alternatives."

"No," McKenzie said. What he would have decided, I still don't know, because someone had found our trail. There were shouts from behind the trees and a burst of noise on the walkie-talkie. The sentry in front jumped into the truck and gunned the

motor. McKenzie floundered ahead, half walking, half crawl-
ing. I grabbed his arm, and we managed the top. I could hear
the truck changing gears. They were going to circle around and
pick us up. Then I heard something else.

"Is that a train?"

"Our only chance," McKenzie said.

"You can't climb that."

"Suppose they want the process?" he asked, his voice tight
and determined as his remarkable will reasserted itself. "Suppose they're not police? They'll try to get it the way Jaeger did.
They'd kill me." He lowered his head and started stubbornly
into the pines. It was hard to help him without hurting his injured
side, and his weight tugged painfully on my back and shoulders.
My legs began trembling with exertion, and, stumbling as we
did, we made a lot of noise. McKenzie slumped against the trunk
of a pine tree. "Where are they?"

"They haven't reached the street yet. Come on!"

"The truck!"

We were almost above the band of pines, but although the
driver braked to a stop, he evidently saw nothing, for an instant
later the machine raced on. Thank God for the lazy love of men
for machines. If he'd run down the street himself, he'd surely
have nailed us. The distant train whistle sounded again, gal-
vanizing McKenzie for a final effort through the meshes of the
thick vines that entangled our feet and concealed stones and holes
and broken branches. McKenzie was wheezing horribly, a
trickle of slobber hanging from his mouth, tears and sweat pouring off his face. He seemed only half-conscious, and I had to half
lift, half drag him from the wet, scratchy grasp of the vines.

Then the roadbed: a mound of loose crushed rock that scattered
underfoot into the greenery. To the right, one stone disinte-
grated, spattering fragments; and the man on the other end of the
high-powered rifle roared at us to stop. His men were crashing
through the trees below. McKenzie fell forward, grabbed the
rails, and heaved himself onto the track. The whistle screamed
as the train rounded the bend and moved toward us. It had to be
the local. I jerked McKenzie to his feet; he cried out, but ignor-

ing his injuries, I clutched him around the waist and, half-crouching, led him over the tracks. The rails began vibrating madly, and the noise of the engine grew like a tornado. McKenzie found his feet at last, and we stumbled out of its path.

"Wave, wave!" he cried, as we fell against the concrete shelter. On the slope were three men half sunk in the vines but moving fast. A corner of the shelter exploded into dust. I raised both arms in surrender, half expecting a shot; but, seeing the train, the men below lowered their weapons out of sight. The local pulled to the platform, its engineer red-faced with fury. He stopped, though, and one of the doors opened. McKenzie and I staggered from the platform to the train, as our pursuers' shouts were interrupted by the high shriek of a long silver express that shot over the railroad bridge and flew past, cutting off warnings, threats, explanations. The engineer released the brake, and we rumbled through the green Nuremberg meadows and into its red-brick suburbs. McKenzie stood gripping the edge of a seat, paralyzed with pain and struggling for breath. The conductor approached, very angry, to lecture us on the danger of crossing the tracks. Every third word was "*verboten*"; I understood little else, but paid for the tickets and explained that McKenzie was sick. He certainly looked it, with his deathly pallor and his staring eyes; and, alarmed, the conductor helped him to a seat. Philip slumped down and closed his eyes. His pulse was still racing but his skin felt cold. I draped my windbreaker around him, and he nodded slightly. "Just need to get my breath back," he said softly.

"How's your side?"

"It's my back now. On fire." His whisper ended in a sharp wheeze.

"Don't talk."

We'd be at the *Bahnhof* within minutes, and we should beat the goons there. Grab a cab and get McKenzie to a hospital? Take a chance on a train out? Go to the police in the station? Call for the U.S. Army again? Who the hell were those guys at the Jaegers', anyway? Everything depended on that. Exhausted, I rubbed my eyes. I should have taken that first-aid course Harry attended; then I'd know what was wrong with McKenzie. He sure looked awful, and, as a distraction from his misery, I stared at the green map in the corridor, a chart of the rail system. When I got up for a closer look, I noticed that there were a number of stops close to Nuremburg. Considering McKenzie's condition, that might be safest. Then call Jürgen. He'd raise hell, but too bad. Move McKenzie north by ambulance. Stash him at the chemical works if he wasn't in danger — or the Honisses' — or some quiet private *Krankenhaus* — and hope the outfit with the automatics wasn't in position to capitalize on his identity. It would be a long shot, requiring a lot of strings pulled just right, possibly a consultation with the police, and a good story for New World. That was a large pre-breakfast order.

"*Nürnberg Hauptbahnhof*," the conductor announced as he passed swiftly through the carriage. Travelers stiff with sleep lifted down their luggage and resumed coats and purpose, while the early commuters folded their papers and took up their places by the doors. McKenzie opened his eyes.

"Make it off the train?"

He nodded.

"I'll check the departures. Whatever we take, we'll get off at the first stop and find you a doctor. O.K.?"

"Yes."

"You're sure? If you have any doubt, we'll get a cab or call a doctor from the station."

"No, no. I'll be all right. Stop asking me."

As his condition worsened, McKenzie grew more determined to proceed. We waited until most of the passengers had squeezed through the doors before making our painful descent. The station was cold and damp, and a chill sooty breeze swept in from the vast open end of the building. Pigeons patrolled the platforms, picking at the crumbs and whirling indignantly up to the ironwork of the curved glass roof as we passed. The head of the tracks was occupied by the usual GIs slouched wearily against their duffel bags and by the food kiosk where travelers stood eating *wurst* sandwiches and apples or downing an even quicker breakfast of *schnapps*. I parked McKenzie on a bench and checked the boards along the row of tracks. A train for Munich in an hour, Stuttgart in forty minutes. Würzburg — I looked at my watch. Five minutes. I ran back, motioning to Philip.

"Train's in. Leaves for Würzburg in five."

"Not a minute too soon."

I looked anxiously around the station, but there were no suspicious groups of men in dark sweaters, no lurking sharpshooter with an automatic under his coat.

"Do you see anyone?" he whispered.

"Nope, not yet."

We reached *Gleis* 4 and walked past the baggage, mail, and dining cars. Philip jerked open the door to a first-class coach, considered the steps for a few seconds, then, clutching the rail, edged up them. During this effort, a confused sound came from the direction of the main concourse.

"Hurry Philip. There's a row in the station," I said, pressing in after him. He staggered along the corridor. The first two compartments were occupied; the next was reserved. I pulled out two of the names and stuck them in my pocket. McKenzie tumbled onto one of the seats, and I pulled down the window shade.

"This should stop at — what's that place — Fürth, the suburb. We'll leave there."

"Safer to go on to Würzburg," McKenzie said, his voice faint and oddly dreamy.

I checked his wrist and found the pulse slower. Was that good? His skin was the color of Camembert. He must be losing blood somewhere. I shook my head.

"Go see who's out there."

I took a cautious look from the door. A couple of railway officials went racing across the back of the station. Something was up, but before I could determine what, the conductor blew his whistle, slammed the last few doors, and the Nuremberg–Würzburg pulled away.

"Someone making a fuss," I reported. "All I could really see were some dark uniforms."

The train rumbled gently into the sunlight; in minutes it would carry us to the Fürth *Bahnhof*, safety, and a doctor. Then the wheels scraped to a halt. McKenzie straightened up quickly, perspiration dampening his pallid face.

"Just the outer station, I expect."

Along the corridor, a door banged before the train again slid forward and picked up speed. The conductor passed, glanced in our compartment and, turning away, tapped once on the glass. Two large gentlemen in dark business suits entered and sat down, the one next to me with a folded-up newspaper which he balanced on his knee. Even though we'd reach Fürth in three or four minutes, the two men were an ominous addition, and my heart began pounding. To avoid looking at them, I raised the shade on the works and power lines whipping past. Did they know us? Fürth was a small station. Should we wait another stop and postpone their move? What did they want? What did it matter — McKenzie was slipping and we couldn't delay. I tapped his arm and nodded. He started to rise, but the older of the two men shook his head.

"Not here, Fräulein."

"Why not?" I asked, standing up. McKenzie leaned his head on the cushion and closed his eyes in resignation.

The second man, younger with dark impatient eyes and rumpled hair, jerked down the shade, then folded back his newspaper to show me a snub-nosed pistol. I sat down, nodding toward McKenzie. "He's not well. He needs a doctor immediately."

"Our credentials, Fräulein," his partner said, opening a leather folder. "I am Kurt Ulrich of the Abwehr and this is Lieutenant Strack. You and Herr Doktor McKenzie are under arrest for espionage."

Chapter 13

A CLATTER OF DOORS, the ring of metal steps, a shout from the baggage cars, the trainman's whistle, and Fürth slipped behind us.

"Espionage?" McKenzie asked.

"You and Fräulein Peters will be charged with aiding known East German agents and as accessories in the murder of a member of the Abwehr."

McKenzie dismissed this information. "I'm a chemist," he said with ludicrous serenity. "Miss Peters deals with everything else. You'll have to talk it over with her." He swayed uncertainly with the movement of the carriage as though on the verge of fainting and added, "I feel terrible, Anna."

"Your outfit raided the Jaegers'?"

"That is correct."

"How did you know we were there?"

"Jaeger's activities have not gone unnoticed. You and Herr Doktor are just a bonus."

I wavered between relief and exasperation. "You might have saved Dr. McKenzie and me a lot of risk and trouble by contacting us in a more conventional manner."

"That was scarcely possible, Fräulein. As it was, several of our men were badly injured." Ulrich looked at his watch before nodding to his assistant and opening the door. "We will discuss your case later. This way, please."

McKenzie rose only to slump dizzily against the window frame, and the lieutenant had to help him out of the compartment. By the time we reached the end of the corridor, the train was already grinding to a halt.

"Get down and go directly toward the back of the train," Ulrich commanded. "Lieutenant Strack will assist Herr Doktor."

We were at a level crossing. The barrier closed off a narrow street lined with trees and privet hedges that hid small brick and stucco houses in their thick foliage. Waiting in the early sun was a black Porsche, the only vehicle in sight. Ahead, the tracks curved slightly, and, with the heavy growth pressing close to the line, other passengers would have difficulty observing our exit. Our arrest had been conducted with both tact and precision: Jürgen Honiss and New World Oil ought to be appreciative.

I walked behind the last carriage and down the track as the train pulled out. As the barriers rose, the Porsche bumped over the rails toward us. Ulrich checked the pockets of my windbreaker, then opened the front door and motioned me in beside the driver. McKenzie waited with the lieutenant, his eyes half closed. When Strack released his arm to get the rear door, Philip crumpled slowly to the ground, his limbs folding up like an accordion. Ulrich and Strack lifted him into the back seat, the driver turned quickly onto a country road, and we sped away. His face grave, Ulrich looked at McKenzie's eyes and felt his pulse.

"He's got to have a doctor," I said. "I'm afraid he's hemorrhaging."

Ulrich nodded. I caught the word "*Krankenwagen—* ambulance — in his orders to our driver. The car radio crackled, and, less than ten minutes later, an ambulance met us at a crossroads. The two attendants flung open the rear doors and rolled out a stretcher for McKenzie, who was quickly transferred, along with our driver. I asked to accompany them, but this was not allowed. The ambulance doors slammed shut, and I felt my previous relief vanish. In its place, a sense of anxiety settled like a bit of heavy weather.

"Where are they taking him?"

"There is a good doctor nearby," Ulrich said. "If he thinks it necessary, he will have Herr McKenzie transferred to a hospital."

I remembered a conversation in Munich. "Jaeger had no confidence in hospital security."

"He would have done better to have had some: his brother was killed in the shooting this morning. But there is no need to worry. Every precaution will be taken with your colleague."

"And Hermann Jaeger? Where is he?"

"Sit in the back seat, Fräulein. We have a great deal to discuss in a very little time. You can proceed, Lieutenant."

Strack started the car, and we left the village for rolling countryside with fields of grain and hops and vegetables. Ulrich took out an elegant black leather notebook and a fat gold pen. He moved deliberately and confidently, like a person accustomed to deference and authority. He looked fit and vigorous, but his main distinction was his air of impenetrable calm, as though he approached all moral questions with complete disinterest. His head was leonine, his features hard, and his hair, gray streaked unevenly with white, was brushed straight back and rather long, confirming my feeling that he was far enough up in the hierarchy to please himself. That might or might not be to my advantage.

"Fräulein Peters, I am sure I needn't point out the seriousness of your situation and Herr Doktor's. I understand you are a person with some experience in these matters. You will realize, then, that both of you face long prison sentences on the evidence already assembled." Ulrich paused to let this register. It did not seem wise to challenge that view just yet. "Of course, any help you can give us will be considered in determining whether or not to prosecute, especially since your company has an important division here. It is in everyone's interest that mutual relations be friendly and cooperative." Despite his calm, almost benevolent manner, I was aware of being weighed in a cold and delicate balance. For the moment, I would ignore his threats.

"You needn't go any further, Herr Ulrich. Dr. McKenzie and I take our predicament very seriously. If we were relieved to see you, it was because we had no clear idea of what was happening at the Jaegers' and every reason to think that we might be killed. Neither of us has any hesitation about cooperating with the West German government."

Ulrich cleared his throat as though he found difficulty digesting this sentiment, and took the cap off his pen. "How did you make contact with the Jaegers?" he asked.

"I first heard about them in a meeting at our home office in

Washington. Dr. McKenzie had been approached at a scientific conference in Frankfurt by Hermann Jaeger, who posed as an East German refugee with a brother still behind the Wall."

"And this brother was supposedly a chemist?"

"Yes. A brilliant one — with a discovery my company was anxious to obtain. I don't understand all the technology involved, but it concerned the separation of oil from seawater."

Ulrich nodded as he continued to write. It was impossible to tell how much he already knew because his features did not betray the slightest reaction. I gave him an outline of events from our first meeting with Hermann in Frankfurt up to the early hours before the raid on the Jaegers' house. I omitted only an account of McKenzie's nocturnal adventure in Munich and the information that the process was, in fact, his own. That might have to come out eventually; I preferred that it not come from me: McKenzie had enough against him at the moment. Ulrich listened carefully, asking an occasional question and pausing to correct his notes on a few points. Unlike some busy men, he made no pretense of coming immediately to the point; more than likely, he had left his mind open as to what was and was not crucial in so complicated a case. His questions showed that he was both thorough and subtle and that, for the present, he had decided not to pressure me. I wondered why.

"We left the house when the firing began upstairs and made it to the street without being spotted. I asked Philip if he felt he could get to the main road. He was afraid that whoever had attacked the Jaegers might turn out to demand information from him as Jaeger had."

"What information exactly?"

"McKenzie is a fine chemist — the head of an important division in our labs. His background in oil chemistry is outstanding, and I've no doubt a lot of commercially valuable information could be elicited from him."

"Yet Jaeger was offering to sell your company a process."

"Yes, so he said. The preliminary material he delivered was excellent. Perhaps he needed information our company had to complete it. Perhaps McKenzie — " I tried to think of a plausible, but not too damaging involvement for Philip. "Well, maybe Dr. McKenzie decided on some sort of financial cut, especially in view of the circumstances, and threatened not to recommend purchase. I don't know. As I've explained, I couldn't always follow the conversation."

"So you told me. Was it his idea to catch the train?"

"More or less. He knew that one can flag trains from those stops. It was pure luck we made it and that the express came when it did."

"And that the Würzburg train was leaving so soon. It would have been difficult to plan," Ulrich agreed.

"Nothing was planned."

"We can stop here, Lieutenant," Ulrich said.

There were rough green fields on either side where dairy cows and a few horses grazed. Strack pulled off the road and eased the car along a dirt track into a grove. From the scrubby growth of bushes and small trees, a pheasant called. Ulrich rolled down his window. The sun had burned off the golden mist, and outside was early summer, although the car still held the chill morning's damp and danger. There was no traffic moving on the road back of us, and we were a long way into nowhere. I realized that nothing was decided, and I wondered what they had in mind for McKenzie and for me.

"Now Fräulein," Ulrich resumed, "you and McKenzie had decided to leave the train at Fürth."

"I felt his condition was too serious to delay."

"What would you have done then?"

"Gotten him to a doctor. I think I would have tried to find an ambulance to take him north to Cologne where our branch office is."

Ulrich was still not satisfied. "And then?" he asked.

I lifted my shoulders. "Everything would have depended on McKenzie's condition. And on who had broken into the Jaegers' and found his passport. I would have tried to get him home and out of the way."

"Suppose Herr McKenzie had not been seriously hurt?"

"We'd certainly have left Nuremberg — probably gone right through to Frankfurt or Cologne."

He thought this over. "You said Jaeger contacted you by sending a postcard to your branch manager's house. How would you get in touch with him?"

"McKenzie always handled that. He would send in an order for a certain type of lens to Jaeger's shop in Frankfurt. Jaeger would reply with the date the item would be shipped — that's when they'd meet. He indicated the place by marking one of those tourist brochures the film companies put out."

"Very well. We will go immediately to Cologne."

At this, Strack started the car and began backing up the path toward the main road.

"I would prefer to stay here until we know how Dr. McKenzie is."

"We cannot consult your preference, Fräulein. We will follow your original plan, including moving McKenzie north as soon as he can travel. The closer we follow it, the better chance we will have."

"Since we are already in custody, it hardly makes sense to follow an escape route."

"You are in custody, but not Jaeger. And if we apprehend him, we will be in a position to look more favorably on your case, Fräulein."

"I should think Herr Jaeger would be heading for the border. He gave it a good try, but without his brother, he's scarcely going to be able to infiltrate any U.S. oil company. The game's over."

"There are the papers he wanted to sell your company. Are they still valuable?"

"Very, but it would be easy enough to pick him up if he attempts to sell them. I can't imagine that his government would take the risk of losing him now."

Ulrich ignored this line of thought. "Tell me," he said, in the same quiet, almost disinterested voice, "how much are these papers worth?"

I explained the original deal and the method of payment.

"Jaeger will undoubtedly attempt to contact you."

"He doesn't strike me as being that careless," I said, unconvinced.

"Jaeger and the doctor who treated his brother escaped this morning by a hidden stair that enabled them to get from the back of the house to the meadows without being seen. In the confusion caused by you and Dr. McKenzie, they escaped, but by the time we reached the Nuremberg station, my men had found the doctor. He'd been shot." Ulrich waited, as though this fact were highly significant.

"There was a lot of firing."

He shook his head, pushing his long hair back with an impatient gesture. "He was not hit by any caliber we carried. He was killed by a pistol shot at close range. Jaeger murdered him."

Hermann was ruthless and unpredictable, but that news surprised me. "Why? What could he gain from that?"

"Nothing — if he intends returning to the East. But if he has something else in mind — "

"I see." Jaeger could live for a while off the money he'd already received from New World, then sell the process and retire from his nasty trade. There was only one flaw — he needed whatever data McKenzie had prudently withheld — but Ulrich didn't know that.

"It's the only possibility that fits the facts and fits what we know of Jaeger's character."

"Yes, he might do that — if the material is genuine and if it's complete. The session with McKenzie the other night suggests that something had gone wrong."

"We will question Herr McKenzie as soon as he is able. In the meantime, we will take you to Cologne where you will act exactly as though you and Herr Doktor had escaped."

"With the idea that Jaeger will contact me?"

"Of course."

"I think New World Oil can survive without his discovery, and I intend to tell them that. Any other contacts with this man can only endanger McKenzie and me and jeopardize the company's reputation. It's out of the question."

Ulrich put away his leather notebook and his gold pen. "You'd better rethink that position," he said.

This time the menace under his calm was perfectly evident, and I decided to investigate its composition. "There isn't a shred of evidence that we knew Jaeger's real identity. As for our trip from Munich to Nuremberg, he and his brother were armed and left us no choice. Dr. McKenzie's condition alone should be proof of that. No fair-minded jury would convict us under those circumstances."

Ulrich's voice stayed flat and quiet, his expression almost kindly, but I didn't doubt him when he said, "It's not a question of a jury. Herr McKenzie might simply die from his injuries. We may have gotten him to the doctor too late. As for you, Fräulein, your conduct so far indicates your dislike of restraint. Were you to try to escape our custody, you would meet with an accident. Under the present circumstances, I believe your company would accept our explanations."

So Jaeger was really important, and McKenzie and that last bit of information were my best hope. "If McKenzie dies, you will lose Jaeger. Jaeger will deal only with him, because he thinks he can manage Philip and because he must hope to get something valuable from him. If I'm to contact Jaeger, you'd better let me talk to Philip first, because without the right information and without McKenzie in the background, Jaeger is sure to suspect a trap."

"I think you place too much stress on a mere supposition. I am curious to know why."

"Look," I said, anxious to avoid dangerous ground, "McKenzie was almost killed. He's got to be protected."

"He will be, once we get his version of this interesting story. Now, your passport and your money, please."

"I'll need some cash for Cologne. I can scarcely stay at Abwehr headquarters."

"Wouldn't you have stayed at Jürgen Honiss's house?"

"No, too conspicuous. One of those little towns below the city — near where the chemical works are — would be better. And Honiss will want nothing to do with this."

"Honiss and your company will give us full cooperation. It's to their advantage to build good will, and besides, if we are successful, New World Oil will obtain that process at a bargain price."

I remembered the man in the park, his blood dripping off a bay hack, and the thin, aggressive doctor watching the chess game, and the sounds McKenzie made when Jaeger had beaten him in the cellar.

"In my estimation, it's cost too much already."

"Then Fräulein, you will be careful and see that it does not cost more. You will go to Cologne, stay there, and begin sending messages to Frankfurt. Sooner or later, someone will be curious enough to answer them."

As far as he knew that was true. If Jaeger had the complete process, if he thought I was ignorant of who had attacked the house, if Philip and I had gotten away, then he probably would try to go through with the deal. He could verify the third, and gamble on the second, but so long as the first condition remained unfulfilled, there was no reason not to go along with Herr Ulrich, at least for the time being. Provided McKenzie was adequately protected, it looked a good deal safer than the alternatives, for I was of no use to Jaeger when he had nothing worth selling.

"I need to discuss this with Philip," I said, not wishing to seem to acquiesce too quickly. "He is the one in the greatest danger. I won't agree to anything until he is safely on his way back to the States." If McKenzie and his precious information were moved beyond Jaeger's reach, I could afford to humor Ulrich. There was a chance we could still extricate ourselves, provided poor Philip kept his mouth shut. That was the problem: the sooner he got home, the better.

Ulrich didn't agree immediately. He seemed to be studying the steep, immaculate vineyards that rose in irregular stone terraces above the Main. Along the water the grass was a bright, fresh green, and on the slopes, the grayish leaves of the vines made delicate patterns above the hard dry ground.

"You have less choice than you think Fräulein, and Herr Doktor even less. One way or the other, you can be sure that he will agree with whatever we plan."

Chapter 14

I CAN'T SAY Ulrich didn't warn me. I can't even say I under-
estimated him: I knew it was mad to try to finesse a man of his
type. Unfortunately, it would have been equally mad to throw
McKenzie and myself on his mercy — assuming he had any.
Perhaps it was merely an attack of the untimely optimism which
periodically makes a hash of my affairs. Perhaps it was just the
consequence of nerves, weariness, and anxiety, but whatever had
prompted me to lie to Herr Ulrich, I now had to play my part until
New World could put pressure on the Germans. I hoped Jürgen
Honiss would undertake that task, but in this, as in a number of
other respects, I was to be sorely disappointed.

We stopped in Frankfurt for some calls Ulrich didn't trust over
the car radio, before continuing to Bonn, where Strack pulled into
the parking lot of the main station. Before us were streets of
handsome stone houses in pale shades of buff, yellow, and gray,
and the Hauptbahnhof, looking like a toy station with its bright
paint and flower boxes. Ulrich, impatiently checking his watch,
might have been an elderly stationmaster surveying his domain.
Punctuality, indeed, seemed his only fetish.

"Do you understand the plan, Fräulein?"

He had gone over it in precise detail. I would pick up an afternoon local and get off at Wessling, just south of Cologne, where I
would stay at the station hotel. I was to contact Jürgen Honiss
immediately and to give him an order for a camera lens which he
would forward to Jaeger from Cologne. This done, McKenzie
would be moved north as soon as possible. There was only one
omission. "I'll need some money," I reminded Ulrich.

Strack, like his chief, had begun anxious consultations with a
timepiece, and neither answered. Then Ulrich pointed to a man
approaching through the parking lot. Dressed in a stained,

open-necked sport shirt and shabby chinos, he struck me as somehow familiar.

"Jakob will take care of all the bills," Ulrich said. "Here he is now. We thought you might be late," he added severely, as the man opened the front door.

"Sorry, sir, the drive took longer than we'd expected."

"This is Fräulein Peters, Jakob." Ulrich turned to me. "Herr McKenzie called you 'Anna,' did he not?"

"Yes, but who is this?"

"This is Jakob Franke. You will be careful always to refer to him as Philip McKenzie."

I realized that Franke was wearing McKenzie's clothes. "You aren't serious!"

"Fräulein, I am always serious. Franke is the best we can manage under the circumstances. Take off your cap, Jakob."

His hair was the right color, and they'd taken the trouble to shave away two patches on either side, to heighten his forehead and to mimic McKenzie's receding hairline. Franke was of roughly the same size and complexion as McKenzie, although no one who knew Philip would ever mistake them for an instant.

"Dr. McKenzie wears glasses," I said, believing it best to stick to factual details.

Jakob produced a wire-rimmed pair like Philip's and put them on. "Plain glass," he said, tapping them. His accent was abominable.

"Well?" asked Ulrich. "What do you think? Remember all we need is someone who creates the same general impression. No one you're likely to see will know Herr McKenzie, except Jürgen Honiss, who will understand the situation."

Jakob put his cap back on.

"No cap," I said. "Philip never wore a hat."

"They are the same size, you see," Ulrich continued. "The clothes fit very well. Have you the documents, Jakob?"

He took out an American passport. It was Philip's, with Jakob Franke's picture inserted. Someone had put in a busy morning.

"His English isn't good enough."

"Doktor McKenzie's German was perfect and in a small town

like Wessling, one speaks German. You will have to be careful, Fräulein, to let Jakob handle conversations in German and to avoid speaking English when you two will be overheard."

Strack smirked as though there was something funny about this prohibition. There was something funny about the whole deal. "What exactly is the point of this, Herr Ulrich?"

"Do not waste my time, Fräulein. You and Herr Doktor escape from a difficult and dangerous situation. You travel to a town near where you have friends and wait until things return to normal. It is perfectly simple."

"It's a waste of effort, because Jaeger won't know where we are, anyway."

"No, but this way we will know where you are — at all times, Fräulein Peters. That is important."

There was no debating that.

"Ah, and one thing more."

"What?"

"Your relationship with Herr Doktor. What was it?"

"None really in the organization. He's head of one of our — "

Strack smirked again, and Ulrich interrupted, "No, personal. Personal. Did you like him, dislike him, go to bed with him?"

"Strictly business. McKenzie — " I stopped myself. McKenzie's preferences were none of their concern.

"Yes, what is it?"

"He's — likable enough in his way."

"Good. That will simplify Jakob's duties."

Strack suppressed a laugh, and I felt myself getting hot with the quick foolish anger that follows fear and stress. "If you want me to cooperate, drop the jokes. And you'd better produce McKenzie."

"You are in no position to make conditions," Ulrich reminded me complacently. "And please stay with Jacob at all times. It would be unsafe for you to be on your own."

With this, he looked at his watch as though for confirmation. "You have the tickets, Jakob? Good. You will have just enough time to get onto the platform. Good-by, Fräulein Peters. We will expect to hear from your acquaintance in Frankfurt."

The soft throb of the local sounded down the line as Jakob and I hurried up the stairs. The sunny street, the trees, the open stretch of track steadily contracted by the oncoming train: I had a momentary glimpse of freedom, quickly shut off by practicality. No one was in the market for heroics, least of all me. We climbed into a crowded second-class car and sat down, Jakob giving me a smile of encouragment, as though to a backward pupil. He had a naturally open and cheerful face, which had not quite achieved the official façade that was Ulrich's distinction and Strack's aspiration. His eyes were sharp and alert, though, and he seemed competent: a promising appearance for a chap in counterespionage but not at all like New World's mercurial chemist. Sitting next to him, I saw how darkly McKenzie's shirt was stained with sweat and dirt and how badly the slacks had been torn. If Philip had suffered a really severe injury, our efforts to escape from the Jaegers could have done him a lot of harm.

For the next twenty minutes, the train followed the graceful curves of the Rhine through alternating bands of industry and agriculture, then Wessling was announced by the smokestacks and gasometers of its large chemical works, and Franke and I exited through a small dark *Bahnhof* to the station hotel. We took rooms as Dr. McKenzie and Fräulein Peters and phoned Jürgen Honiss before venturing up a street lined with the cramped little shops of small towns to find a cafe.

"Do you know how Philip is?"

"They have taken him to a hospital. They had to give him blood."

Franke ordered lunch, two plates of schnitzel with noodles on the side, that promised to provide a good deal of ballast for an empty stomach. There was absolutely nothing more to say, and we ate in complete silence and left.

"You will buy paper," Franke directed as we walked toward our rendezvous with Honiss.

"And you will buy some clothes."

"These are Herr McKenzie's clothes," he protested, a trifle defensive about his disguise.

"They are a little too much."

"What does that mean?"

"I mean Philip wouldn't have wanted to look so conspicuous. You look like a fugitive from a chain gang."

"Herr McKenzie is — ah — what is the word — sloppy?"

"There are limits even for McKenzie." They had paid some attention to Philip, then. I wondered for how long. If they knew too much about his activities, all hope of deceiving Ulrich was mere delusion.

We bought some writing paper, and Franke selected a checked sport shirt at a shop in the center of town. Past the modern square around the Rathaus, he pointed to a park adjoining a small brick church. The grass and flowerbeds were set off by shrubs backed against an imposing stone wall. Behind this, a steep flight of steps led to an open field along the river. Upstream were clusters of blocky gray factories; downstream an explosives plant owned by our German subsidiary. Sandwiched between these two industrial areas was open land and a dairy farm. A dirt road ran through this pastoral intervale, and a couple of cyclists and pedestrians with shopping bags could be seen heading out from town. A breeze blew from the open country on the far bank to rustle the long marsh grass in a drainage ditch and to complicate the maneuverings of a kestral hovering over the meadow. When we crossed a rough stone-and-earth jetty, we saw a man in a business suit pacing the stony shore. Jürgen Honiss was giving a very unconvincing imitation of a man on a lunch hour ramble.

"Guten Tag, Jürgen."

He had not heard us approach over the sound of the wind, and he turned sharply, jerking his head in response to my greeting. All trace of his usual friendly courtesy expunged.

"Herr Ulrich?" he asked.

"His associate, Jakob Franke. Herr Franke, Jürgen Honiss, manager of New World Oil in Germany." Jürgen preserved a pained expression, which deepened at the mention of New World. I realized I could expect little help from him.

"Did Ulrich tell you about McKenzie?" I asked. "I'm afraid he's been seriously hurt. You will have to inform Gilson immediately."

Jakob shook his head vigorously. "Who is this Gilson?"
Jürgen explained in German.

"No. Everything must go as normally, Fräulein."

I shrugged and tried to catch Jürgen's eye. "Herr Honiss has
some responsibilities to our company," I said meaningfully.
Jürgen pretended not to hear. I tried another tack. "Ulrich will
arrange to have McKenzie moved to Cologne as soon as he is able
to travel. You will have to make arrangements to have him flown
home. He must have the best possible care."

Jürgen looked at the agent for confirmation. He was really in a
bit of a panic. After another exchange of remarks in German, he
said, "Herr Franke tells me McKenzie will be moved to a private
clinic under guard."

"That's right. He is in some danger so long as Jaeger remains
at large. That is why the home office must be informed. We
can't allow our undercover friends here to try anything tricky." I
spoke fast, too fast for Franke's weak English. He frowned.

"There must be complete cooperation between your company
and our department," he said. "No one else must know of Herr
Doktor's injury."

Jürgen reassured the agent at some length, while I stood turning over pebbles with one foot. Whatever they'd told Honiss had
been effective. Either they had something on him, or his fear was
simply the result of his perfect picture-postcard life. Perhaps this
uneasiness in the face of official displeasure was the inevitable
obverse of that glossy, handsome smugness which distinguished
the entire Honiss establishment.

"There are limits to how much you can expect from either one
of us," I said sharply, "especially since Dr. McKenzie's condition is uncertain and since you have taken my passport without
any kind of legal process. Tell him that in German, Jürgen."

Franke did not care for the translation, and Jürgen was finally
forced to address me directly. "I do not like these irregularities,
Anna. I did not like the matter in the first place. Do not expect
me to contravene the orders of my government to retrieve a
scheme which seemed improper from the very first."

"There is nothing improper or unusual in wishing to purchase a new technological development," I said with more heat than conviction. "There is something improper about allowing a clandestine government agency to manipulate people's lives for its own purposes. Following orders is not really good enough — as you of all people should realize." That was a low blow, but at the moment I said the hell with good will and international understanding.

Jürgen's strong, handsome face turned brick red with anger, but all he said was, "I've explained my position." He could stand on his dignity with the best of them.

Franke took out a pen. "We will send a message to Herr Jaeger," he said. "That is why we're here." Jürgen and I glared at each other over the ruins of our former cordiality, then I sat down on the grass and wrote an order for a wide-angle lens for a Leica. Jürgen translated this to Franke, who shook his head.

"You must warn him," he said. "It must be believable."

"Something like, 'I am writing this at the direction of Herr Franke of the Abwehr'?"

Ignoring this pleasantry, he spoke to Honiss, who explained that the warning must be couched in terms of the lens.

I redrafted the note. "How's this: 'To avoid breakage, please ship this order with the utmost care. We do not wish the problems of earlier shipments to be repeated.'?"

Franke looked at Jürgen who nodded. "It is all right."

I addressed an envelope to Jaeger's camera shop in Frankfurt.

"Can it get there tomorrow?" I asked.

Jürgen looked at his watch. "There is a chance, if I drop it at the main post office right away."

"Very good," said Franke, and Jürgen strode away toward the explosive works where his beautiful BMW was collecting a film of dust from the construction work at the rear of the plant. Franke and I headed in the opposite direction for the park.

"You put him in a bad position," Franke said.

"He's been well paid for it."

"You cannot expect him to be disloyal, Fräulein."

"There are different kinds of loyalties."

"Women pay too much attention to personal loyalties."

"And men to abstractions justifying anything?"

This was either uncomfortable ground or Franke's English was already over-extended. I was just as glad. Sex differences elicit more hot air than a balloonists' rally. We climbed the steps back to the park and returned to the hotel for three and a half of the most boring days of my life, in which the tedium of absolute inactivity and Franke's surveillance were broken only by increasing anxiety. I was annoyed because they wouldn't let me call Harry, and as I had anticipated, we heard nothing from Jaeger. We also heard nothing about McKenzie, and I was ready to abandon my waiting game when a summons arrived from Herr Ulrich.

Chapter 15

I HAD FAILED TO APPRECIATE the extent of Ulrich's subtlety; his manipulation of others' psyches was as precisely calculated as his timetable and left as little to chance. By the time Strack picked me up in the car, Ulrich must already have had the entire scenario in mind.

It was raining that day, and as we drove toward the hospital, the cathedral spires kept reappearing out of the mist, black and enormous above the plaza cleared by Allied bombers a generation ago. We crossed the Rhine to the suburbs and eventually parked behind a modern, three-story building with picture windows, trim balconies, and the familiar hospital smell of disinfectant and anxiety. Strack led me upstairs to a suite well off the main corridor, where a bored plainclothesman sat drinking coffee behind a desk. In the room beyond, McKenzie stared through the drizzle at the cathedral rising blue-gray in the distance like a cutout pasted against the sky.

"How're you doing, Philip?"

He looked oddly small and flattened down under the white covers, and when he turned, I saw he wore a weak, faraway expression. "There's a bit less of me than when I saw you last."

Strack had said that they'd removed McKenzie's spleen. There was also some other, minor, damage and several broken ribs. "The doctors say you'll be up and around pretty soon. Are you in much pain?"

"Not now. I wouldn't care to go through the past few days again, though."

I pulled a chair close to the bed. "Can we talk here — or do you think there's a mike?"

McKenzie made a gesture of indifference. "It doesn't matter."

"I've been after Honiss to pressure them to send you home.

Ulrich and company won't let me call the Washington office."

McKenzie gave a faint smile, as though such activity were quaintly amusing — trivial politicking fit only for one's salad days. Strack had mentioned that Philip was seriously depressed; that seemed an accurate assessment.

"You'll be safer at home. You've had a severe shock."

"Is that the diagnosis?"

"Yes."

"My doctor is a thorough materialist."

"A fellow scientist."

"Do you know why I did this?" McKenzie asked after a moment. "The whole thing, I mean?"

"I know you needed money."

"I needed what money could buy — or what it tries to, anyway."

There were drapes at the window, pictures on the walls, a vase of flowers: the room was an eavesdropper's paradise.

"Careful," I warned.

"It doesn't matter," Philip repeated.

"You'd better watch those impulses."

"Which?"

"The self-destructive ones to let everything go and to say nothing matters. Materialist or not, your doctor's right. You've had a nasty jolt, but the situation's still salvageable. Remember Frankfurt, please. There's no point in making things worse for both of us."

"Oh, you'll be all right. You're a survivor. Do you know why?" He pulled himself up on the pillows with sudden animation.

"Don't tire yourself, Philip."

"You have brakes on inside. I used to. I used to live like Herr Ulrich — by the clock. Don't trust him, incidentally; he's liable to go off in crazy ways. Funny, you know, my work was the most important thing for years and years. School, labs, universities, papers, journals — with intervals, of course." He gave another little smile. "But nothing serious, nothing at all serious, until — "

The wind shifted, sending rain in spatters against the window and blurring the view of the city and the spires in a hail of wet, expanding circles.

"Until Andy Ravelle," I said.

Philip nodded.

"An expensive item."

"Not just that. Probably I could have swung the money. Oh, I thought it was important at the time. I'd still like a cut."

"You can always use money," I agreed.

"It was the — is 'glamor' too cheap a word? I think it is. It was the freedom of breaking away from what I had always done, of being completely in control of events. Of being more important than my own discoveries," he added with a touch of bitterness. "I was ready to 'live.' Of course, that's an illusion, isn't it? One always lives essentially the same way."

I held a similar philosophy, but this wasn't the time to encourage abstract reflection. "This particular bit of living isn't habitual with me," I protested.

"No." There was a pause. "But it comes to the same thing. We live by necessity, impulse, and habit. The proportions differ, that's all. Most of us can't manage by will and calculation."

"Only monsters can."

"Beautiful monsters. Andy is a beautiful monster."

"Herr Jaeger is an ugly monster."

"I've lost everything," McKenzie said in a faint voice.

"Don't say that. You can't afford self-pity just yet, you're not strong enough. You're going to get better, go home, and reconstruct what you supposedly 'learned' about the process. You can even find someone else to ruin yourself over."

"I couldn't work again. What lab would — "

"Shhh. They don't need to know, do they? We got our money's worth from what Hermann sold us originally. New World will have to be satisfied with that." I leaned closer. "Ulrich made me write to Frankfurt — the way you used to contact Hermann — with an order for a camera lens. No answer. We'll wait them out. Get you home. Report to the big boss that Jaeger was a phony and that the deal blew up. Then you can recapitulate the experiments in light of what you talked over with Wilhelm, and *voilá*."

"There'd be some awkward questions about the results."

"You were having emotional problems when you worked through the experiments the first time. Undergoing a religious crisis or tax troubles — whatever you like."

"You'd have to say something. You weren't keen on dealing with Jaeger in the first place."

"Right, and they refused my advice and ignored the evidence which suggested that the deal was a phony from the start. So. I don't owe them a thing. What about it?"

"That's nice of you." He sighed and closed his eyes. When he didn't speak for several minutes, I got up, thinking that he was asleep. Then Philip opened his eyes. "There's only one problem," he said. "Ulrich knows the whole story."

I sat back down.

"I appreciate your offer, though."

Philip was, no doubt, too depressed and sick to understand the extent of this disaster. I wished I was similarly anesthetized. "How did that happen?"

"I told him. It seemed the best thing. He rather blamed you, you know. Past history or something. I had the impression you were going to take the rap, and I was going to turn over the scientific work and get off. That's what it looked like anyway."

"Well, this way we hang together, but thanks for the company, Philip."

"Oh, don't credit chivalry." He gave a soft laugh. Talking about it actually seemed to cheer him. "They had some heavier artillery in reserve. A thirteen-year-old in Frankfurt." He shrugged. "Nothing to it as a matter of fact, but Ulrich showed me the deposition."

"We could have fought that."

"I couldn't face it," he said, and I thought that was probably true. He looked as though he'd run through his remarkable reserves. "And then there was Andy."

"I've met Andy," I said.

"Yes?"

"He seems able to take care of himself."

"Yes, he always was. But just the same — " McKenzie rummaged disconsolately through some memories. "Nothing came of it, you know, until he was older."

I remembered the evening we'd spent along the river with Honiss and his family. McKenzie liked children and had a knack with them. Ulrich had found a sensitive spot when he charged Philip with betraying a child's confidence. Perhaps that was the thrust that had uncovered his real betrayal of his colleagues in the New World lab. Ulrich was subtle, all right, and he had the same killer instinct as Jaeger, although on an infinitely more refined plane.

"I told Ulrich the whole story."

"I didn't," I said ruefully. "He'll want my head."

"I've been writing out the missing material for him," Philip continued. "It will be finished by tomorrow. I'm afraid I'm going to lose the rights to my discovery entirely."

"Ulrich wants to use that material to attract Jaeger, so there's still a chance we can get his copy and pass if off to New World as the real thing."

"If they snare Jaeger."

"We'll have to see they do," I said with the horrid cheerfulness of sickroom visits. McKenzie deserved better, but he was exhausted enough for one day. I pushed away my chair, uncertain how best to leave. Finally I shook his hand gently. "If you get home ahead of me, say nothing, huh? Have amnesia, all right?"

He nodded.

"Good-by, Philip."

As I closed the door to his room, I heard him say, "Keep well." I also heard the click of a recorder switching off, but then I'd expected that. Strack led the way into the corridor and down the back stair.

"Herr Ulrich is waiting to see you," he said.

We drove to a lot in the open grassland along the river and parked beside the black Porsche. Ulrich emerged and motioned me into a steady drizzle which seeped through my sweater and spotted my slacks. He was wearing a raincoat. It was a good illustration of our respective positions.

"So Fräulein Peters," he said, before waves of displeasure washed over me like a tide. His silences could be intimidating.

"You and Herr McKenzie have wasted a good deal of our time, Fräulein," he resumed when I made no comment.

"Sitting in Wessling with Jakob Franke isn't my idea of a holiday."

"You are incurably frivolous, Fräulein. It is time you thought seriously about your situation."

"I've been thinking about nothing else, I assure you. I am under no obligation to you. It was your business to apprehend Herr Jaeger, not to harass me, and it's hardly my fault you chose the latter. I did what you ordered, but I was not obliged to help further and I'm not inclined to now, considering your treatment of Dr. McKenzie. He's in bad shape, mentally, and physically, he's not fit for work at all."

Far back in Ulrich's eyes was rage, but none came to the surface. He was holding that in reserve, perhaps, and it struck me again that the cordial Germans are an inscrutable people.

"Herr Doktor has cooperated with us. Sensibly. There were a number of charges possible against him. Espionage was the most logical, but in his case it proved unsatisfactory. Like certain other scientific minds, he finds espionage a concept beyond his comprehension. It was necessary to use something else. Fortunately, when I questioned your relationship with him, your reaction set us on the right track."

He strolled farther onto the soggy green verge. "My work, Fräulein, is composed of psychology and analysis. Analysis for data collected, psychology for persons to be apprehended. When one is correct on both counts, the results are predictable. It is a matter of knowing what people want — or don't want — to happen."

"And you think you know what Hermann Jaeger wants."

"I have what Hermann Jaeger wants, and you will give it to him. Hermann Jaeger wants the material Herr Doktor McKenzie has conveniently provided. You will see that he comes for it.

Otherwise your situation will be impossible. The bluff is over, Fräulein. McKenzie was, admittedly, in a susceptible frame of mind, but you could be put in one, too. Some of our jails are not very nice. There have been unfortunate incidents with prisoners, lately. With regard to the law, you see, we are people at an awkward transitional stage. I assure you, many things are possible." He gave a flicker of a smile, which was the residue of rage transformed into dominance. "But I don't think I need threaten you. You work on different principles, don't you? You would like Herr Jaeger's — or more properly Herr Doktor Mc-Kenzie's — discovery. It can be arranged."

"Not without exposing Philip. I'm not sure he can take any more pressure and I'm not willing to destroy him for a few extra cents per share for New World Oil. We all have our limits, Herr Ulrich."

"But it is not to our advantage to expose Herr Doktor, Fräulein. Far from it. That would raise questions. Besides, if Jaeger suspected we had Herr Doktor, he would have no reason to contact you, would he? You're not apt to buy something you already have — not even to deceive your corporation — when you and Herr McKenzie could simply split the sale price yourselves. I suspect that possibility was considered."

"It came up for discussion."

"*Ja,* and Jaeger would certainly have thought of it. No, Fräulein, there is only one circumstance that will attract Jaeger now, and we must act quickly to provide it."

"What's that?"

"McKenzie's death."

"You don't mean to — "

"If Herr Doktor dies," Ulrich explained calmly, "Jaeger's papers are worth a fortune, provided, of course, that McKenzie did not leave another copy. Jaeger will need to find out about that and when he hears of McKenzie's death, he will certainly contact you."

I was speechless, and Ulrich indulged in a soft, disagreeable laugh. "One gets tired of the past here, Fräulein, and tired of people unable to forget it. Do you think that you are dealing with the Gestapo? Herr Doktor's 'death' need not be fatal for him — if you are careful. Ane you will be, won't you? *Ja*, I thought so. Good. Wouldyoulikemetotellyouhow Herr Doktor will die?''

"And how you can insure that Jaeger will learn of it."

"That will be my worry, but I think our friends in the press will take care of us, if we do something sufficiently newsworthy. Now, then, you and Jakob Franke go walking every afternoon. Today you will go walking for a longer time than usual — a hike fairly far along the Rhine, perhaps. When you return to the hotel, Herr McKenzie, that is to say, Jakob, will take sick and collapse, preferably in the street. We will have to check the train schedules. The ideal time would be when there are lots of people in the station area. The police will be called and an ambulance — we will arrange all of that — and a photographer will happen to be on the scene. It will be in the news that Herr Doktor McKenzie, a distinguished American chemist, collapsed and died suddenly while on a holiday in Germany. You will see," Ulrich concluded as he turned back to the car, "how nicely it will work — so long as you follow our directions exactly. And Fräulein, please be assured that now you have no choice but to do just that."

With his warning, he opened his car door and switched on the transmitter. A few moments later, he returned with final instructions. "You will time the Doktor's collapse with the four-o-three from Cologne, Fräulein, and you and Jakob will need to be near the front door of the hotel so that everything is visible from the station platform. Understand?"

"Suppose there's a real doctor around — or that the local police arrive before your squad?"

"We will alert the local authorities. Should there be a doctor on the platform, you will have to keep him from accompanying the ambulance. It should not be difficult since you speak such a limited amount of German. A misunderstanding would be quite plausible."

Ulrich checked the time. "Buy something on the way back, Fräulein. Remember you've been out shopping this morning."

Then he nodded to Strack, who started the car, and we were dismissed.

This plan was put into immediate action, and, less than two hours later, Jakob Franke and I went tramping along the narrow path toward the explosive plant. He carried the large black umbrella indispensable to his scientific persona, while I shrank within the folds of a new rain poncho and tried to avoid the wet gusts blowing on the stiff breeze off the river. Dairy cows were huddled in dispirited groups near the battered shrubs of their pastures, and the apple trees overhanging the thoroughfare ran with water. For this disagreeable day, we had strict orders not to be back in Wessling before ten to four. Even Franke, normally a jaunty, even-tempered chap, was downcast. He was taking the doctor's impending demise quite seriously, because he was afraid his wife would recognize him in the newsphotos. There'd be hell to pay, he said, if she thought he'd been spending the past few days at a station hotel with me. He had my sympathy. If you put aside McKenzie's disaster, there were some humorous elements in our situation, but I was not sure Harry would have found them funny, either. It was not a day for seeing the lighter side of anything.

We walked under the overpass linking the main part of the explosives works to its outer buildings and entered a stretch of overgrown land, poised between swampy meadow and scrubby forest. There, the trees offered protection, but the wind continued to play havoc with Franke's umbrella. When we spotted a small open shed, he suggested that we hole up for the afternoon. We sat on the damp earth, watching the rain on the river and talking disjointedly in a mixture of English and German about our upcoming theatrical venture, its inevitable domestic consequences, and the inexplicable ways of men in charge. I learned that Franke had worked for Ulrich for three years and that he took a kind of perverse pride in the exactions of his chief. More about Herr Ulrich's psychology was not obtainable, however, except for the fact that it was dangerous to cross him and fatal to make him an enemy.

I found myself reviewing these points as we returned down one of the back streets near the station. Franke was absorbed in rehearsing the scene to come, a prospect he had confessed he found embarrassing.

"It's five to four," I said, and we quickened our pace, arriving at the entrance to the station. Franke stopped and leaned against a street lamp, his hand over his heart, while I feigned honest concern. He twisted his head to look at my watch and achieved an expression of genuine pain.

"Not time yet?"

"Better wait until we hear the train."

"I want to get this over with," he whispered.

I took his arm and we moved slowly toward the hotel, Franke stopping every few paces as though to catch his breath. "You're doing fine. Very authentic."

"I'm thinking about my wife."

We were almost at the hotel, when the train rumbled in on the southbound track. I started toward the door, but Franke gave a theatrical groan and dropped to his knees.

"What is it, Philip?" I asked. Then louder, "Are you all right? No, wait! I'll help you."

He sank to the pavement with a look of disgust as his left arm disappeared into a puddle of dirty water. On the station platform, a couple of curious passengers interrupted the rush to the exit. They stood, uneasy, balancing briefcases and shopping bags, uncertain if they should get involved.

"*Helfen Sie mir*," I called. "*Können Sie mir helfen?*" and under my breath, added, "For goodness sake keep groaning."

One man, more decisive than the rest, stepped off the platform and began picking his way across the tracks, while in the doorway of the hotel, the receptionist appeared.

"*Ein Krankenwagen, bitte, und ein Arzt. Schnell*," I called to her.

The hotel door slammed. The man from the platform puffed his way up to the street level and spoke rapidly in German. Franke answered in a faint whisper, punctuated by gasps. The

Good Samaritan was not a physician, however, and Franke and I were left in the wet by a growing crowd of sympathetic, but fortunately, quite helpless bystanders until two of the local constabulary came racing down the street, followed shortly by an ambulance. Franke was bundled into a blanket and onto a stretcher, and as he was being lifted into the back, a thin-faced youth in a leather jacket began snapping pictures.

As usual, Herr Ulrich's timing had been impeccable.

Chapter 16

THE LATE EVENING NEWS carried a short notice about the sudden death of a visiting American petrochemist and the morning papers obliged with pictures and stories, all distinguished by their tactful omission of New World Oil administrator, Anna Peters. I read through the articles in the small apartment over Honiss's garage, and the next day a postcard from Hermann Jaeger promptly appeared.

"That's it, then," I said to Ulrich.

He took the card, studied it for a moment, and nodded. "He hasn't changed his tactics."

"What is that place?"

"The Porta Nigra? A Roman gateway with an overlay of Romanesque. A wonderful piece of military architecture, Fräulein, with an interior court to trap anyone who managed to pass the outer gate. An example of foresight."

This ingenious edifice was blackened with the soot and dirt of the ages and bereft of its accompanying city walls. "Not the best of omens," I said.

"On the contrary. He is following the pattern. He is gambling that even if the meeting is a trap, we won't risk a shoot-out around crowds of visitors. It is reassuring to know how his mind works."

"Don't forget, either Jaeger or his brother surprised your man in the Englischergarten."

"We will be prepared, Fräulein, but I should warn you that more than one meeting may be required."

"I didn't sign on for an entire campaign."

Ulrich knew my rebellion was a mere gesture and remained blandly reassuring. "You will be safe enough at the Porta Nigra. Tour buses arrive every half hour or so. But by the same token, he is not going to want to conduct his business so openly. Even if he trusted you completely, I doubt he'd bring the papers to the first meeting."

"He may not even want to sell them."

"Take the money and keep the papers? That will depend on how desperate his situation has become. You will be safe, though, I assure you. We may be able to follow him from the Porta Nigra and arrest him away from the crowds, but we will have to be careful. He has a good nose for police."

"Have you gotten the money?"

"Yes."

"Enough?"

"I cannot guarantee, Fräulein, but for a man on the run a million marks is a lot of money."

"In addition, I think we should offer him the same deal as McKenzie."

"Which was?"

"The cash was the downpayment. More would be funneled through a Swiss account and a percentage kicked back — in this case, to me."

"Herr Doktor signed his own warrant," Ulrich said with a sigh.

"He wasn't entirely trusting. He withheld some of the data."

"You couldn't do that. You don't have any hold over Jaeger."

"My position is weaker, but I think he will expect some sort of proposition. He may be suspicious if I don't demand a share."

Ulrich considered this. Unfortunately, greed lacks a chronometer. "Very well, Fräulein, I wish these negotiations to seem genuine at all cost. I will leave the discussion with Jaeger to you. Strack will bring the money and McKenzie's notes this afternoon."

"I'd rather not take the papers. I'd hate to put temptation in Jaeger's way."

"And where would you leave them? Jaeger will notice details like that. You would have been in contact with your company — must have been to obtain the extra cash — but you could hardly have told them the whole story, could you? Even if

Doktor McKenzie were dead, the facts remaining scarcely put you or the transaction in a good light."

I was being rigged out as a large, slow-moving target. "I don't like the idea."

"Fräulein, the operation must be planned to the last detail," Ulrich said. Like Jaeger, he was running true to form, and after his careful briefing, I began to wonder if his reliance on timing and on detail did not make him just as predictable. If so, my chances were not enhanced. Still, McKenzie's demise and its aftermath had gone smoothly enough. Following Ulrich's orders, I had nipped away from the hospital and kept out of sight. Would I have done that under ordinary conditions? Perhaps not, but so far as Jaeger was concerned, I had to look like a smooth operator who'd conned a bundle from New World Oil and was set to finagle even more. On one thing, Ulrich and I agreed: the more convincing I was in this role, the safer I was going to be.

I looked at my watch, then consulted one of the timetables that sprinkle the interior of German trains; I was picking up Ulrich's habits. The train was due in Trier by midafternoon. Two of his agents were already waiting in the hotel opposite the station and more would be deployed around the Porta Nigra. There was, Ulrich had said, a fair chance Jaeger would be in custody by nightfall, but I rejected the bet, principally because of my knowledge of Jaeger and even more of McKenzie. What could have attracted McKenzie to Jaeger? Only that shared streak of recklessness which in both implied a capacity for surprise and for decisiveness. That I should come to Trier with money, possibly with what was even more valuable, the completion of McKenzie's discovery, was essential. That I should meet him at any one time or place was not. I began to feel uneasy about traveling alone, and the pressure of the case, stuffed with Deutsche marks, and the papers was not reassuring. Possessing the money, Jaeger would have a free rein, and he'd already killed one man, injured a second, even abandoned his brother. Disinclined to be the next victim, I began studying the timetable in earnest. Koblenz was a good possibility — a seven-minute stop — but it was more than an hour up the line from Trier. The only other halt of any duration was Cochem. Four minutes. If I lost the train, I'd miss the rendezvous with Jaeger, and I didn't like to think about Ulrich's reaction.

When the train pulled in, I was waiting at the door with the briefcase. Outside was one of those warm, hazy days peculiar to river valleys, with the sun a radiant spectral presence behind the clouds. The train had gone to the very end of the long, bare platform, necessitating a sprint back past the porters loading baggage, past the plump, officious conductors, past the food kiosk with its big round clock ticking off the seconds with jerky motions of a thin red hand.

"Wo sind die Schliessfächer?" I asked, searching for the lockers.

The porter pointed toward the steep stair leading under the tracks to the station proper.

"Rechts" — right. Right? We were on Track 4 — it wouldn't do at this stage to come up the wrong stair. A man with a huge suitcase and a cane edged grunting down ahead of me, while an anxious matron leading two little girls blocked the other side; no doubt they were rushing to catch the train for Trier. I squeezed between the children and hurried down the slanting corridor to the main room with the ticket windows.

No lockers. Turn right: the station cafe, smelling of grease and sausages. I doubled back. If I couldn't find them in the next few seconds, I'd have to forget the idea and run for the train.

"Schliessfächer?"

The trainman pointed back toward the tracks.

I circled the waiting area, dodging a school group on an outing, and finally spotted the sign tucked behind a newspaper stand. Down the narrow hallway, the first bank of lockers was completely filled, and my watch, informing me I had less than a minute, stimulated the peculiar panic of missed trains. Farther, around the corner, there were some large, empty lockers. I flung the case into the first of these, slammed the door and dropped in two marks, before I realized I needed five pfennigs more. I rummaged through my change. I had over a million marks but no pfennigs. Then I remembered buying an ice cream at the Cologne station. Left pocket? Right pocket. Five pfennigs.

Money in, key out. Check the lock. My watch said thirty seconds left, and I tore along the corridor, up the stairs, and down the platform. The stationmaster had his watch out and his flag up when I reached the last car. The whistle sounded. I wrenched open the door and went rocking down the corridor as the train accelerated. My heart was still in overdrive when I stepped over the long legs of a pair of Swedish travelers and resumed my seat by the window. Herr Jaeger's money reposed in number 512 in the Cochem *Schliessfächer;* all that was left was to hide the key.

I consulted my suitcase but it was not helpful, being merely a cheap vinyl number with no convenient false bottom or secret compartment. My few possessions proved similarly ineffectual. There was no monster jar of cold cream, none of the feminine paraphernalia so useful in thwarting curious males, all but the essentials having been jettisoned. In the washroom, I upended my bag. Out fell a room key from the station hotel, abandoned along with McKenzie. It would have to do. I broke a fingernail and bent the towel dispenser prying loose the key ring. The locker key went on the room tag, and the room key and the label of number 512 went out the window. Then I enjoyed the scenery along the Mosel until the train pulled into Trier, and we exited to a humpbacked station standing against steep vineyards.

There was a fair crowd on the platform, mostly tourists laden with suitcases and souvenirs headed for the big airfield in Luxembourg, and I made my way slowly through the crush to a passageway lined with travel posters and grime. I had gone only a few steps when a porter appeared to take my suitcase. This was unusual.

"Nein, danke," I said.

He grabbed the handle of the suitcase. Beneath the shadow of the porter's black cap, I recognized Jaeger's snub nose and bottomless dark eyes. He smiled, a perfect caricature of servile cordiality.

"Walk straight ahead," he said.

"This is not the Porta Nigra."

"We must be extra careful. You, especially; I am armed. Turn right ahead. I will carry the luggage."

Ulrich might have an agent in the station, but it would be dangerous to look around. We walked toward the *Schliessfächer*, as though Jaeger were helping me check my suitcase, and through a door behind the lockers to a sorting room for parcels and rail deliveries. Jaeger stuffed his porter's cap in his pocket and folded his coat over his arm. A squat, tanned, muscular man, he seemed too ordinary to be dangerous — until one studied his eyes. I was impressed again by their preternatural alertness. Surely that, rather than mere strength or intelligence had accounted for his longevity in a dangerous profession. Wariness, quick reactions, and a complete absorption in his own survival had so far enabled him to retrieve whatever his impulses endangered. I stumbled slightly on a loose strip of linoleum. Understanding Jaeger's ability was fine, but it didn't change the fact that the man beside me was born for violence. I was scared.

The depot opened at the side onto a cobblestone yard for trucks to unload. We walked down the building to the rear door of the station restaurant, where a beer truck was parked, kegs and cases of empties on the curb before it. Jaeger motioned me into the driver's side and followed with my luggage. Then the motor roared, and we jounced over the stones to the street. Jaeger turned sharply off the main drag, and within a few minutes we were driving on a winding road through the vineyards. At the crest of one hill, he steered onto a narrow track behind a stretch of terracing and stopped. Far below were the dark stone buildings of Trier and the silver serpentine of the Mosel, edged by rust-colored cliffs. The only thing following us was a cloud of dust.

"You might have been watched," Jaeger remarked.

"Possibly. I don't trust Honiss."

"Is the company still interested in the process?"

"Very much so."

He pocketed the ignition key and produced a compact, efficient-looking pistol. "How much?"

"A million marks — as a downpayment."

Jaeger's brilliant eyes revealed nothing. I noticed a mole on one cheek and thick bristles of hair in his nostrils. "And then?"

"If the material proves satisfactory, the original deal holds."

"According to McKenzie, the material is incomplete!"

"Philip had begun to reconstruct the document before he collapsed. If we pool our resources, we will have something very valuable."

"And where is Herr Doktor's reconstruction?"

"Safe. As is the downpayment, of course. I didn't suppose you would be prepared for an exchange on our initial meeting."

Jaeger searched through my suitcase, then helped himself to my bag and repeated the process. He read the label on the key to the station hotel before dropping it back in the bag and beginning to tap irritably with the gun barrel on the steering wheel. He was debating whether to knock the money out of me and settle for a million marks or to play along and hope to fatten his Swiss account. Or perhaps he would try to grab everything and approach another oil company. But that would require time, and time was undoubtedly a commodity Herr Jaeger was running short on.

I forced myself to speak. "Of course, if the company accepts the discovery, I expect a share of the profits."

"Herr Doktor and I had agreed on a percentage."

"I was thinking of half, since I will be providing half of the document as well as taking some of the risks."

He gave a derisive laugh. "What risks?"

"You, Herr Jaeger, are a considerable risk in yourself."

This seemed to please him, I was not wrong in thinking there was a strong sadistic streak in his character.

"Remember that," he said. "In fact," turning to face me, "what is to prevent me from demanding the money now — and Herr Doktor's papers as well?"

"Nothing at all, except you'd be pretty conspicuous going to get them. I am not a complete fool, Herr Jaeger." To my ears, that lacked conviction, but he continued.

"And what's to prevent you, Fräulein, from forgetting to pass on the rest of the cash?"

"There will be legal papers to be signed. So long as you keep your side of the bargain, New World Oil will think the discovery is legally yours. So long as I cooperate with you, you will continue to give New World the legal rights the company requires. It's simplicity itself — provided you have someone inside the company willing to keep quiet about the circumstances and to bend a few rules.''

Jaeger thought this over. His fingernails were cracked and dirty as if he had, indeed, been working as a porter or a truck driver for the last few days. He looked off into the golden haze along the river. Two thousand years ago the outpost legionnaires must have looked a lot like him: squat, tough, and predatory. I had never warmed up much to the Romans, but that hardly mattered. If I'd misjudged this particular adventurer, I was going to be sharing the Rhineland's sandy soil with the bones of the legions.

Then Jaeger spoke. "If you step out of line, you're dead," he said, very soft and cold, with the curious caressing tone that had teased McKenzie. Jaeger enjoyed power and no mistake.

"An understandable condition."

"Good."

He stuck the pistol into his shoulder holster and pulled out a map of the city, on which the square of the Roman town was clearly visible. "Tonight at nine, you will drive around the old city. Here." One short thick finger traced the outline of the boulevards that ran along the remnants of the walls. At the base of the square, beside the river, the streets fed into the main road north and south. "You will circle the town as many times as necessary, until I meet you."

"Where?"

He hesitated, and I stopped breathing, but he'd already made up his mind.

"I will signal to you. You will pull over and stop. We will exchange cases. As you say, it's a matter of cooperation." His mouth twisted into a thick unpromising smile.

"All right." Perhaps I'd been reprieved, after all, and I fought to keep Jaeger from detecting my relief. He operated on a delicate alarm system which I mustn't trip. "I'll have to see about a car."

Jaeger started the truck, backed it recklessly to the edge of the terracing, then sent us careening down the steep hillside. We crossed the tracks and drove through town toward the river.

"Walk back past the Porta Nigra. There's a car dealer there," he said when he stopped.

I almost fell out of the truck, I had gotten a cramp in one foot. "Tonight at nine."

"Until then, Fräulein." Jaeger gunned the motor. The truck disappeared along the road to Saarbrücken, and I started toward the soot-colored Roman gate, abandoned at the crossroads like a set left by some traveling theater.

Chapter 17

AT THE DESK the receptionist gave me a funny look, and when I opened the door to my room I saw why. Lieutenant Strack was sitting tipped back in a straight chair with his feet on the bed, and Ulrich was standing with his hands behind his back and his head bulled forward like Churchill at a Blitz site.

"Where have you been, Fräulein?"

I banged the door shut and threw my suitcase on the floor. "I don't care for this wallpaper," I said, feeling lightheaded, "too orangey."

"You are an hour and fifty-seven minutes late."

Strack wiggled his long nose and registered his opinion: "*Bier*."

"I hope you haven't been drinking," Ulrich said quickly, and for the first time, I detected a certain anxiety in his tone. So he was human. I'd begun to wonder.

"Do I look drunk? I should look scared. I've just spent an hour talking with Hermann Jaeger."

Even that smartass Strack straightened up.

"What about the money, Fräulein? And Herr Doktor's papers?" Ulrich demanded.

"Locker five hundred twelve — *funf hundert zwolf* — at the Cochem *Bahnhof*." I threw the key to Strack, who lunged for it, settling his chair on the floor with a crash.

"The *Schliessfächer* are a bit hard to find. Around the corner off the main lobby. We'll need the money by nine. Also a car. I don't think I can rent one without a passport."

"Where is Jaeger?"

"Last I saw, he was driving a beer truck in the direction of Saarbrücken."

"A beer truck? What kind of beer truck?"

"A big, brown beer truck. I don't know what kind." Storm clouds gathered around Ulrich. He was right; obviously I should have noticed, but it had been a rough afternoon. I sat down on an uncomfortable stool designed for suitcases.

"The name, Fräulein."

I shook my head. "It had a design on the side. A red spot, I think."

Strack reeled off half a dozen names.

"No, a short name. An English name, maybe."

"Union," Ulrich suggested. "Dortmunder Union?" A haze of white letters fluttered in my memory and disappeared. "Could be. Sorry, I can't be sure. I only saw the outside for a minute."

"Where did you leave him?"

"At the bottom of the street that runs past the Porta Nigra to the station. He turned right onto the north-south route."

"How long ago?"

"Twenty minutes, maybe twenty-five."

Ulrich waggled his head like an angry turkey. "Too long. You should have called us immediately. We might have picked him up on the highway."

"How was I to know where you were? I nearly got shot this afternoon, in case you missed that. If I hadn't checked the cash at Cochem, I would have been."

Unlike some Olympian minds, Ulrich's was impervious to criticism. "Alert all surrounding police units, Lieutenant."

"Jaeger's armed," I warned.

"Send someone to Cochem," he added to Strack, "and have Robert come in. You come back, too, as soon as you can."

Strack left, and the level of irritation dropped slightly but perceptibly. For some reason, I had focused all my dislike of the business on him.

"Now, Fräulein, from the beginning. What happened?"

I recounted the afternoon, ending with Jaeger's plan for our meeting. Ulrich got a map and had me trace the route I was to follow that night, as well as what I could remember of our ride in the truck. "We were up in the vineyards, that's really all I can say. My mind was on what I should tell Jaeger."

"Yes, observation would be difficult in those conditions." Ulrich took a half turn around the room. "He must be suspicious."

"Yes, but his greed has gotten the better of him."

Ulrich nodded. "Herr McKenzie presented him with a great temptation: the opportunity to set himself up in a major U.S. oil company. And the best part of it was that both your company and his contacts in the East would be paying him. Thanks to your foolish chemist, Jaeger could move into big time espionage almost without effort. And now, of course, having cut his lines to East Germany, he doesn't want to lose everything he gambled for."

"I think now he always intended to kill McKenzie."

"Certainly. For both of you, it is just a matter of time with Jaeger."

"That's reassuring."

"There is no point in my lying, Fräulein," Ulrich replied imperturbably.

"Perhaps you'll get lucky and spot the truck."

"Jaeger will undoubtedly have abandoned it. Nonetheless, we will do our best."

A gentle knock on the door preceded a man with white hair and a young face who entered as smoothly as if he moved on casters. "Can you drive a shift car, Fräulein?" Ulrich asked.

"Only with difficulty."

He fired off some orders, and the man glided out. "Robert will see about your car. He'll leave it on the street."

Half a block away a building was being framed, and the heavy thunder of the piledriver cut through the warm afternoon like the beating of a sickly pulse. It was an unnerving sound.

"I'm willing to go through with this, Herr Ulrich, but only up to a point."

"And what is that point, Fräulein?"

"I don't want to meet Jaeger alone. I've used up my luck with him."

"If the timing is right, we can intercept him. We will know where you are at all times, of course. An electronic signal in the car will do that. We can minimize the risks."

"Jaeger's survived a long time."

"Survival isn't everything, Fräulein."

"Neither is money."

"No, but there is more to Herr Jaeger than simple greed," Ulrich said thoughtfully. "I've had him under observation for one reason or another for quite some time. I think there's a lot more to him than that."

But what else there was, he did not elaborate, and at five to nine, when I unlocked the blue Volkswagen sedan, I was none the wiser. In spite of Ulrich's thoroughness, intercepting Jaeger would still be a matter of chance. He was no longer driving the Union beer truck, which had been found in Konz, a village just north of Trier. Strack had been dispatched to investigate that incident and to question the machine's proper driver, who'd been found unconscious shortly after the alarm had gone out. Like Ulrich, I felt less sure of Jaeger's motivation than I had before. Maybe there wasn't any — just random folly and viciousness: the brutality with which the driver had been attacked seemed needless and, worse, unprofessional.

Nightfall had brought a close and ominous atmosphere, like a musty blanket flung over the city. I wiped my sweaty hands against my slacks and started slowly down the Theodor-Heussallee with its narrow strip of parkland, past the Porta Nigra, and down the dark, tree-lined streets to the river; a few blocks in the fast traffic along the Mosel, then up the Sudallee to the rotary at the top of the Roman square. Across the bare concrete lanes, powerful spotlights picked out the arches of the Baths, dark and corroded like the ribs of some half-devoured leviathan. Beyond them, a long stretch of wall was still intact, and the headlights shone through the gray trees to its pink and buff bricks. I reached the *Bahnhof* again without any sign from Jaeger. Perhaps he wouldn't show.

I repeated the circuit around Trier's ancient, slightly shabby, streets. It was a sympathetic town in some ways, without the spotless efficiency of the sleek Northern cities or the fat smell of wealth of a Frankfurt or a Munich. Architectural epochs stood next to each other, Roman, Romanesque, Medieval, Baroque, Victorian, Bauhaus, like cards riffled in a pack; and around them drifted the faint weariness of ancient places, neglected for Progress. I eased the sedan into the dwindling traffic on the main road, tempted to floor the accelerator and see how far I could run. Somewhere Robert or Strack or even Jakob Franke, now resurrected, would be tracing the sound of the bleeper affixed to the car. I turned up the Sudallee again, wondering how much longer I'd have to circle. A smell of gas lingered in the car and made me feel slightly sick even with the windows open. From dreading a signal from Jaeger, I became impatient for it: I wanted to get finished with the whole rotten business.

I had almost reached the rotary on the third circuit, when a big car sliced into my lane, its taillights flashing. I felt a prickly band of tension run across under my lungs before a deceptive rush of adrenalin set my heart jumping. The lights kept signaling, and the man at the wheel drove straight through the rotary and turned off onto a side street. I followed slowly to give Ulrich's people time to notice that the pattern had been broken. Where the street dead-ended, the driver turned his car around, then roared past me, flicked his lights, and parked. It was Jaeger all right, and I drove to the end of the lane and turned, carefully reversing the car twice to delay the inevitable. If Ulrich's men were nearby, they would block off the street, and I didn't want to be caught beside Jaeger in that trap. His car edged forward; he wanted to see what was moving on the main road. What in hell was keeping them? Then Jaeger's door opened and he turned, sitting half out of the car. My headlights gleamed on the pistol steadied neatly on his arm. Ulrich was late, and after a few seconds, I realized that I had no choice but to keep my appointment.

"Get in the car," Jaeger said, rising as he spoke to train the gun on me.

On the seat was the leather case he'd brought to the Palmengarten the first time we'd met. I laid the briefcase with the money on top, and he sat down heavily and flicked open the catches. The light from the dashboard washed over the deep contours of his face, picking out his features in sulfurous yellow. I could smell sweat and beer. There was no time to delay; I had to get away from the car before Ulrich's men arrived.

"The papers?" I asked, drawing out the bottom case. There was hoarse fear in my voice and Jaeger knew it.

"Open it and see, Fräulein. I am sure you will want to check them carefully." Jaeger was an unstable substance, as unpredictable as a tiger, and I had gotten too close.

The case held a leathery smell and a fat handful of writing paper densely covered with mathematical symbols and close-set paragraphs of almost illegible German. "I will have to take your word about this."

Jaeger riffled another packet of bills without answering. I hoped Ulrich had not done anything clever with the money. Then I depressed the door handle. "If this is the real thing, you will hear through your bank in about a week."

Even five seconds more, and I would have been out of the car, but whoever made the mistake made it five seconds early. The police radio squawked only once, but Jaeger had lived too many years with such sounds to miss it. He moved by instinct, faster than I could have imagined. The car lurched forward, banging the door shut and flinging me against the cases. Jaeger wrenched the wheel, taking the corner like an iceboat and providing me a glimpse of red and blue lights and the two-toned police cars angled like teeth across the street, before a bullet shattered the rear window, and I ducked. An engine roared ahead of us, filling the car with the explosive white brightness of oncoming headlights. Jaeger stabbed the brakes, fishtailing the car across both lanes, then rammed onto the narrow sidewalk. The concrete wall of a garden scraped the fenders before he swerved back onto the street, jolting off the sidewalk with a crunch that shredded the undercarriage. The police car skidded past on our right, as we threaded the narrow gap and went rocketing forward.

The rest of the squad cars had been stationed ahead, in a lane beyond the amphitheater. Their orders were not elaborate: they just pulled squarely across the street and began putting bullets into the front end of our car. Fragments of glass glistened on the windshield like snowflakes, and despite frantic efforts, Jaeger lost control and hit the accelerator in desperation. We leaped the curb, crashed across the gravel lot on the left, and shot for a low wall and a mound of ruins. The one functioning headlight showed the flesh-colored Roman brick, the grassy mounds above, and the thin bars of a rusted metal grill that smashed apart with a high twanging sound when the car hit it. We were flung forward onto the dashboard. I felt something wet on my face, then Jaeger grabbed my arm and hauled me out the open door. "Take the cases."

He fired twice at the lights and noise behind us, then trained the pistol on me. "This way," he said, forcing me behind the thick brickwork and along the shadowed curve of the inner wall of the arena. After the blinding lights, the vast stone-and-earth construction was sunk in darkness, and I stumbled on the grass. Jaeger caught my shoulder and pushed me ahead until I touched the wall. Both ends of the amphitheater were pierced by wide, sloping ramps, and, through the trees growing at the far end, I could see a few winking city lights. Jaeger pointed toward the opening. Behind us came the screech of twisting metal and the roar of a straining engine as they tried to move the car from the entrance gate. Someone was running on the grass-covered terraces, and flashlights appeared in the vineyards higher up. We weren't going to make it.

A circle of light began prowling the wall ahead of us, and Jaeger jerked me into an alcove fronting a barred cell. We flattened ourselves against the ironwork that had separated — what? — from the prisoners or gladiators waiting on the sand. The cage gave off a peculiar odor, noticeable even to one panting for breath. There was a smell of unimaginably old dust and an unsettling suggestion of something else as yet indefinable. As the light swept across the opening to pass to the next alcove, we made a break down the deep shadows of the wall past a crumbling tunnel like the entrance to a football stadium. Then flashlights began blinking in the far end of the amphitheater, and we knew we were trapped. Jaeger froze, his eyes bright and fathomless as an animal's, and even in the blackness, I could see his teeth set in a faint smile. When he laid the pistol against my neck, the cold metal amplified the pulse in my jugular a dozen times, and the sound of my own blood filled the bowl of the arena. Then he gestured with the weapon. "Over there," he said, "quietly."

A dozen feet away, on the sandy grass, was the outline of a metal railing. I hesitated, but Jaeger pulled me down into a crouch and hauled me after him. From above the trees came the throbbing racket of a helicopter that cast a pencil of white light down the terraces to form an expanding spot on the floor of the arena. "This side," Jaeger hissed.

The metal railing enclosed a flight of stone steps, running steeply into the earth. At the bottom was a door. Pushing me to one side, Jaeger set the pistol against the lock and fired, the clatter of the helicopter absorbing the sound. He kicked the door open and demanded the money. "There is a walkway," he said, as I handed over the case. "You must go carefully." Then he shut the door behind us.

We were in the vast substructure of the amphitheater, the network of tunnels and cells and animal cages, prop rooms, equipment rooms, and storage areas that formed a structure below the sand almost as vast as the terracing. The helicopter hovered above like a dragonfly, its searchlights powerful enough to illuminate the few square skylights set into the floor of the arena. Their faint greenish light disappeared in inky water where, yet deeper, submerged rooms and tunnels reflected the beams from their pale stone walls. A catwalk of rough boards zigzagged over these flooded rooms. The stone and earth arching above was shored up here and there by modern pilings, and through the gloom, I could see how this upper level stretched into the vast darkness of the farthest corners of the arena. Then the helicopter clattered off to sweep the outer walls, and we were left drowned in shadows and in the smell of the amphitheater, the smell, even here over the water, of dryness, age, desiccated bones: the smell of death.

"From the other side we can reach the exit ramp."

"They will search here too, surely."

"Then Fräulein," he began, but his words were cut off by the racket of the chopper's return. He did not need to explain. If we were finally cornered, I would cease to be useful. Ulrich was right. For me, as for McKenzie, coexistence with Jaeger was infinitely precarious.

We started along the catwalk. I steadied myself on the wooden rail, picking up a trail of slivers from the rough planed wood as we moved deeper under the arena floor. I was suffocating with the horror of enclosed places, as though the great weight and depth of soil and brick above were sinking into my chest. Even more than of Jaeger, I was afraid of being entombed in this close grave. The skylight ahead was flooded with an eerie glow, and I noticed that there were bulbs set in the ceiling to light the passage. I forced myself to look down into the water. Shallow directly beneath the walkway, it was deep farther on, where the floor had fallen through to the level below. The catwalk bent around a piling, and before the helicopter light shifted, I saw the stair. I had to get out into the open air, and, gasping for breath, I started quickly forward in the blackness.

"Not so fast. I will shoot."

"The 'copter's gone. We can get up the stair now."

I turned to face him, but continued edging toward the door.

"No! We must wait."

"They will come down here."

"They will think we got out. They will send most of their men after us and leave only a few to search this passage. We will make our move then."

I was farther from Jaeger than at any time since I had gotten into his car. When they searched here they would turn on the overhead lights. Had he forgotten that? And when the lights went on, he would certainly kill me. Perhaps he was waiting for that. Perhaps he had no real hope left and had settled on this as a proper terminus. I risked another step backward.

"Stop there, Fräulein, or I will shoot."

"A waste of ammunition. I can't hurt you."

"I will shoot just the same."

"They will hear the shot."

"Not under here."

We were both breathing heavily in the bad air, and the cavern enlarged this feeble rustle until it became the panting of lions. I was aware that Jaeger was closing the gap between us.

"Perhaps I will shoot you anyway," he said. He spoke softly, his normally harsh voice smooth as oil. Instinct screamed for the stair, the door, the night sky. I lifted the case with the papers and set it on the rail of the catwalk.

"If you shoot, you will lose the papers. Even incomplete, they are valuable."

I heard him move in the blackness. He was very close. He might miss with one shot, but he would hit me before I managed the door. I took another step back and leaned my weight against the rail. The water was my only hope.

"I am holding the case over the railing," I said, loudly, to cover the sound as I slid my leg onto the guardrail. I wasn't sure I could do it. To be shot in the water. There would be rats. The water might be too shallow. The insidious odor of the place was growing stronger, and breathing that air was like inhaling cowardice; I couldn't do it. Jaeger hadn't moved again; he was hesitating, like me, listening to determine exactly where I was. Then the helicopter came racketing toward us, and I knew that Jaeger was waiting for the lights and sound. I must do it now. The machine came on like a locomotive, like a grotesque angel of oblivion, and as its beam washed the farthest skylight, I flung the case at Jaeger and myself over the rail and into the foul, ebony water.

A sharp pain across my back, an explosion of water and sound, then cold, enveloping, suffocating, black wetness. Shock forced all the air from my lungs, and in terror, I thought I was drowning. I thrashed desperately in the water; one foot grazed bottom, and I thrust my head up for breath. Jaeger sent a shot spattering nearby, and I dived, scraping one knee on a hunk of rough masonry, then, finding deep water, plunged downward. The light from the chopper overhead cast a glow into the murky pool in time to prevent me from swimming headlong into a wall. There were shots behind me, and I slipped through a doorway into complete blackness. I had entered nothingness: no sound, no light, no air. I saw the trap and turned, but the light had shifted and I could not find the entrance, my sense of direction stymied by the black fluid filling up that grave of beasts and gladiators. Panic roared in my ears; I had very little air. Must have air. Must be an opening. I stretched out my arms and felt around me: my hands touched walls on both sides. I was in a narrow tunnel leading deeper into the ruins, and I had to find where the roof had collapsed before I ran out of oxygen. I kicked hard and shot forward only to strike my head on the stonework; the tunnel slanted downward. There must be an open room. I could feel each individual brick and stone. Suppose the doors were lower, the tunnel deeper. Suppose I missed them. Suppose all these rooms were intact. Suppose I found one and couldn't get out of it. Suppose this darkness was the last thing I would ever know. But there had to be an opening — overhead, perhaps — if I could only see. My lungs began burning, rebelling, demanding the fatal fluid. On each stroke, I ran my hands along the walls, seeking the openings hidden in the dark. Suddenly, I touched stone in front of me and despaired. There was water in my mouth, sickening and choking, then a faint brownish glow appeared in the depths to my left and I drove toward it, squandering the last of my strength. My arm broke through the water and I hurled myself, gasping, into the precious air. I had come up in some ruined chamber, and feeling the outline of a wall in the murk, I clambered up on a fragment. Jaeger was forgotten: I balanced against the rough slimy stones and vomited the filthy water. My nose and throat were on fire, and I gulped down air to fill up my ravenous lungs.

I had forgotten the skylights along with Jaeger, but he was not so distracted, because his first shot hit a piling near me: I heard the wood splinter. He was still out there in the dark. He was mad. He still intended to kill me. He was going to come after me, wading crazily through pools and over walls, splashing through the dangerous, disgusting shallows until he cornered me in the untouched caverns at the farthest end of the arena. I slipped back into the water, but nothing on earth would make me submerge into those depths again. I crept behind the masonry to find shallow water that only reached my knees. There were open pits in the floor, though, and I stepped into one, chilling my heart until I grabbed the wall and pulled myself back from extinction. I clung to the brickwork, listening for the sound of Jaeger's approach.

Then, sudden as lightning, the electricity came on, and with the lights, a terrible cannonade of sound from both stairwells. Heavy automatic fire ripped across the structure, reverberating through the caverns; and clods of earth dropped from the ceiling as though the whole great ancient bowl was about to cave in. There were screams above the fusillade, a high, terrible descant, and some frantic, injured creature floundered in the water. Then came voices, and the chopper whirred overhead, and boots clattered down the stone steps. I straightened up slowly to see a low, crumbling maze of rooms, filled with lagoons of stagnant water and spotted black by treacherous sinks where the flooring had collapsed to the tunnels below. Men with guns were standing on the catwalk, and I was close enough to smell the blood. They had killed Jaeger.

"Over here! Don't shoot! *Helfen Sie mir!*"

A round white light dazzled me, before settling gently onto the wall like a moth. I leaned against the stones. It was very cold and my knee seemed unusually stiff. Someone jumped off the catwalk and waded forward, a light held above his head. We sloshed back over the top of the sealed passage and under the string of bare lights. There was a red mess on the catwalk and below it, drifting on the muddy water, the white pages of McKenzie's discovery opened like Hadean waterlilies.

Chapter 18

I LAY ON A HIGH METAL TABLE fighting the emotional aftershocks from the events in the arena. The bare fluorescent tubes in the ceiling hurt my eyes, and I had a mangled knee, a skinned back, a badly bruised ankle, and five stitches across the top of my forehead. The doctor had sewn up the cuts, X-rayed the joints, and shot me full of serum to fight the tetanus, typhoid, typhus, and other bacilli feared lingering in the amphitheater sump. He was now pondering the X rays hung over a lighted rack. The rack was set too low for his considerable height, and he had to accentuate his marked stoop and hunch his long wrinkled neck like a turtle to examine the pictures. My physician did not inspire immediate confidence. His tweed trousers sagged like a vaudeville comic's, and his white coat had been washed and ironed to a shiny thinness. His white hair was scant but long, and it, like the rest of his person and, indeed, like his well-hidden office, was in a state of advanced dishevelment. Nonetheless, he was a cheerful old bird, for now and again he would shuffle to the table and do something excruciating to my injured leg while mumbling reassuringly, *"Gut, sehr gut, Fräulein."* Then he would return to contemplate the X rays while pain made the ceiling lights waver in and out of focus and the taste of the water in the amphitheater made its nauseating return. I would have traded all his antibiotics for a good slug of brandy or a large glass of clean white Mosel.

He pottered over to find an extremely sensitive spot on the side of my knee.

"Ask him why he keeps saying 'good' when it hurts like hell," I told Lieutenant Strack.

The doctor beamed paternally when this was translated.

"He says there is nothing broken and no real damage."

"Just pain."

Strack was not sympathetic. "You're lucky," he said.

"Not lucky, resourceful. A damn good thing, too."

The doctor beamed again and began to wrap my knee. *"Sehr gut, Fräulein,"* he said, patting my shoulder. For some reason, I felt like crying. The quacks who advocate confronting your fears are crazy; terror isn't healthy, and there's no vaccine for its after-effects. Then the doctor winked and sent Strack out. I sat up, catching a glimpse of myself in one of the mirrored cabinets. I was wearing a borrowed sweater and a khaki blanket. They complemented the suggestions of disaster provided by the tape across my forehead and the padded bandage around my knee, but they wouldn't catch on for Fall. The doctor rummaged in a closet, retrieving a dusty bottle of white wine which he opened and poured into two large glasses. He tasted one, pronounced it good, then handed me the other and told me to drink it slowly. It was the nectar of the gods. Smiling, the doctor left the room for a moment, to return with a couple of rolls of uncertain origin. He insisted I try these too, and although dry, they had a soothing effect. I felt the atmosphere of the amphitheater begin to recede. *"Danke schön, Herr Arzt."*

"Langsamer, Fräulein, langsamer," he said, pouring a little more wine into the glass before shuffling away to his outer office. I climbed off the table and tried out my legs. They were sore and stiff, but the doctor was right: everything was operational. I struggled into a dry pair of slacks, and I had just finished this painful process when there was a peremptory knock on the door.

"Come in."

Herr Ulrich appeared carrying a stout cane. He looked as completely untouched and in control as ever. "How are you, Fräulein Peters?" he asked.

"Apt to survive, but I'm going to have a knee like Joe Namath's."

He helped me back to the table. "Dr. Groh is a fine doctor. Very reliable."

Emphasis on reliable. I drank some more of the wine. "I'm inclined to agree."

Ulrich studied me for a moment before deciding I could go the distance. He took out a brown envelope and dropped it in my lap. "This is for you: part of Herr McKenzie's manuscript. He should be able to reconstruct the rest."

I opened the flap and recognized Philip's large, undisciplined hand. This version was in English. "The other papers were lost?"

"Yes. Jaeger's brother favored a fountain pen for some reason. Everything was ruined in the water, and I think we must assume that the Jaegers destroyed McKenzie's first manuscript."

"I would think so. What about the money?"

"That was recovered."

"Jaeger insisted on carrying it himself."

"We observed that." No doubt Ulrich had seen the mess on the catwalk, too.

I held up the envelope. "Who else knows about this?"

"No one of importance. We told Honiss only what he had to know."

"Namely that he had to cooperate."

"Do not underestimate patriotism," Ulrich replied sententiously.

"Next time, I'll appeal to his better nature. But thanks for the papers; they may make matters easier for McKenzie. Incidentally, I'd like to see him as soon as possible. Certain things have to be settled before we go home."

"Yes, I can understand. Tomorrow, if you're able. The doctors say his prognosis is good. Of course," Ulrich paused and pivoted to glance over my X rays, "Herr McKenzie may have something new in mind."

I recognize a hint when I hear one. "Such as?"

"You will see him tomorrow, Fräulein," Ulrich said firmly, "but in the meantime, I would not make any plans for Herr Doktor. You will see. Can I help you down?" he asked with something approaching solicitude. "We know a quiet hotel outside of town. Robert will take you there and tomorrow he will drive you on to Cologne."

"All right."

He handed me the cane, and I limped to the door. "I believe, Fräulein, I have arranged things so there will be no repercussions. I hope I needn't convince you that that is important."

Shock waves were still rippling through my system. "There have been quite a few repercussions already," I said.

Ulrich nodded. He wasn't hostile, just monumentally indifferent. With him, duty conquered both impulse and sentiment; he was the triumph of order. "It will be in your interest to see that there are no more." I didn't doubt it. Then he opened the door. "Good-by, Fräulein Peters," he said politely. Robert sprang up from a seat in the foyer, and we exited to the mild night and a fast Mercedes.

Jürgen Honiss was not glad to see me when I showed up at the Cologne office. I wasn't happy to see him, either. The adrenalin had gone down but the bruises hadn't. I just wanted to see McKenzie, find out when he was coming home, and leave.

"What has happened, Fräulein Peters?" Honiss exclaimed.

"I was in an auto accident the other night. Fog on the autobahn. Nothing serious."

Honiss gave me a sour look. "Another car? This isn't going to do our insurance record any good. You'd better give my secretary all the details."

"Not my car, fortunately. I'm sure Ulrich will square everything with the rental agency."

He looked relieved. "Well, that's good. You're flying home tomorrow, I suppose, since we've made arrangements."

"That depends."

"Herr Ulrich assured me you could leave any time. He said you'd been a great help." Honiss dropped his voice to a more intimate level. "The successful completion of this project may be important for New World Oil. I think we can expect the utmost governmental consideration from now on."

"I'm glad to hear that, because there is still Dr. McKenzie to be taken care of."

"Herr Ulrich has that in hand," Honiss said as a flicker of nervousness passed over his handsome face. "I will tell you on the way to the clinic." He stuck some papers in his pocket, before pushing the intercom button to tell his secretary we were leaving. "It would have been better if you'd met me there," he remarked. "There might be some questions." His gesture encompassed my modern disaster appearance.

"No problem." Ulrich had devised a traffic accident report. "I was told to give you this. You're to mail it to the home office, because I'm entitled to workmen's compensation and company insurance."

"Very efficient," Honiss admitted. "Come this way; my car's at the back."

He relaxed somewhat when we were out of the office, but he still didn't mention McKenzie's future.

"How's Philip?" I asked, finally.

"Coming along."

"Have the doctors said when he can go home yet?"

"That's what I want to talk to you about, Anna. Dr. McKenzie isn't going home."

"Why not?"

"For one thing, he's officially dead."

"That's inconvenient but correctable. McKenzie did your government a service. They can certainly push the right papers around for him and give the American authorities some explanation."

"Dr. McKenzie has agreed to another plan. They haven't told me everything, but Dr. McKenzie — and you, too, for all I know — was evidently involved in some fraudulent scheme. Am I right?"

"You were explaining the plan, Jürgen, not asking questions."

"Very well. Dr. McKenzie's going to stay dead. Ulrich's offered him another identity."

"He must be crazy."

"That's a matter of opinion. I've questioned McKenzie at some length. He agreed of his own free will, because it seems his career will be ruined anyway if he returns to the States. I understand that there are a lot of questions being asked at the home office, and for everyone's sake I feel he's made the right decision."

"And you let him? Without telling Washington he's still alive. I can hardly believe that of you, Jürgen."

"A man has a right to his own life, his own decisions."

"Surely it has struck you that Philip, despite his extraordinary intelligence, is not entirely normal."

"Well, I've heard he's — "

"Emotionally he's on a roller coaster. He's not completely responsible for either his actions or his decisions. When I saw him last, the diagnosis was severe depression. Correct? Now he's off on a harebrained scheme which you and the German government want to exploit. I can't go along with that."

"I think you'd better. It's all settled."

"It damn well isn't settled. We'll call the home office and get this straightened out."

Jürgen shook his head. "You'd better talk to Dr. McKenzie before you do anything foolish, and you'd better read these."

He handed me a couple of letters and cables from Bertrand Gilson in D.C. I soon realized that McKenzie had been judged in absentia: the corporate brass wasn't mourning his death, because awkward questions had been raised about the venture and about the workings of the laboratory division Philip had headed. There was growing suspicion that the Jaeger papers weren't genuine, and, all things considered, Dr. McKenzie's timely coronary had gotten everyone off the hook. Everyone, that is, but me, who'd had the bad taste to anticipate my superiors' conclusions. But that was minor. Good relations with the German government, which Honiss had so confidently predicted, were going to be worth more than Jaeger's dubious patent.

"But you haven't told them Philip's still alive."

"They really didn't want to hear that."

"And the patent?"

"Ulrich's official line is that Herr Jaeger was killed, and the papers lost."

"I see."

Honiss gave me a sharp glance. "That's correct, isn't it? I mean, assuming that discovery ever did exist, it's gone now?"

I folded up the letters. Gilson and company were running scared, and, as a result, we underlings were about to be sacrificed to that great god, Appearance. If so, New World didn't deserve anything from us. "That's right, Jürgen. The circumstances of Jaeger's death make it certain."

"I never approved of dealing with a man like that."

"It appears Washington now agrees with you. The hospital's just ahead. You can drop me off; I'll find my own way back."

"Are you sure?" he asked, braking with noticeable eagerness. "The less company involvement, the better. Dr. McKenzie is in room four hundred."

"I'll find him. This is all right, Jürgen, I can manage." I was able to walk, but the blocks were longer than I'd remembered and, during the hobble to the clinic, I had plenty of time to ponder my future. When I reached his room, I thought about Philip's. He was sitting up in a bright, striped robe, looking pale and thin but obviously improved.

"Hello, Philip."

"Herr Schloder, please. I don't think you know him, do you, Anna?"

"We've got to talk about this Herr Schloder business."

"I doubt you're the one to advise me. You don't look as if you've been taking your usual pains with yourself. And a cane! Premature senility threatens."

"I'm in a mood to be serious this afternoon, Philip, and we'd better get right to the point. Why have you let Ulrich and Honiss talk you into this crazy proposition?"

"It suits me. A lot of other Herr's would not have, but as soon as they mentioned Herr Schloder, I knew it was for me. He opens up possibilities, don't you think? No debts, no ties, no recriminations — no jail." McKenzie's eyes danced. He was entering one of his manic phases for sure.

"Have they threatened you with prison?"

"Not in so many words. Jürgen's first-rate at the oblique threat, the unprovable insinuation. But we're going to screw him anyway."

"I hope you're speaking figuratively."

"Not your type, either, huh?" McKenzie's smile was like sun over ice; his archness hid gall. "I haven't told him that we can still have the process; that it is all mine and safe right here." He tapped his forehead.

"Right. No one knows that but you and me. And Papa Ulrich has returned this." I handed him the envelope with the manuscript.

McKenzie flipped through it, then took a box of tissues, removed the ones on top, and pulled out more papers covered with figures. "There it is, complete and worth a fortune."

"To somebody, no doubt."

"Why not to Herr Schloder?"

"New World would prosecute sure as sunrise."

"Someone they'd never heard of?"

"Come off it, Philip. If Herr Schloder or whoever you're going to be produces that, how long do you think it will before New World smokes you out? If you want to be Schloder, you can't have Jaeger's discovery. And if you want the discovery, you're damn well not going to be able to remain Schloder for very long. No cover in the world would stand the kind of publicity that patent'll bring. And you know it."

"You just want New World to have this," he said nervously.

"I'm rapidly becoming indifferent to New World's interests, Philip, but I think you and I might still profit from this mess."

McKenzie remained silent, his eyes uncertain.

"I don't know what New World will do because the heat's on back home, but if this is the real thing, I think they'll be inclined to overlook what happened and, probably, to throw in enough cash to keep you from exposing the incompetence that allowed you to pull the deal in the first place. You won't get what you wanted, but you won't have to throw your life and talents away as Schloder, either."

McKenzie shook his head. "No, it was an all-or-nothing scheme. I don't plan to return to any New World lab."

"But what will you do?"

"Just what I have been doing. Schloder's a qualified chemist. I have a job waiting for me, which is more than you can guarantee with all your optimism. As a matter of fact, it sounds — "

McKenzie was interrupted by the arrival of an attractive blond intern who made a few jokes, asked a few questions, filled out his chart, and departed. I gave McKenzie a quizzical look.

"You have a suspicious nature," he said with mock indignation. "Besides he's straight as a string."

"How do you know?"

"As they say about prices, if you have to ask, my dear — "

"My apologies."

McKenzie shrugged, and in the gesture I saw the despair underneath his flippancy. "Schloder's nothing to you one way or the other."

"It seems a waste, that's all."

"Of course it's a waste," McKenzie's voice was sharp. "That's why I refuse to do it halfway. I don't want to give creeps like Gilson my work. I never wanted to. I couldn't stand that corporate crap. I took their money, I intended to cheat them. Too bad I couldn't pull it off. I'm unrepentant."

"That's the first hopeful thing you've said."

"Since you have a kind of primitive sense of justice, I thought it might shock you. I was spared that encumbrance, fortunately."

And that's why he had been cast adrift. He was as amoral as Jaeger, but entirely lacking in deliberate viciousness. That made his flight from himself ironic, for there was nothing stable in him to flee. "What about Andy? He's going to think you are dead."

"It won't matter to him. It will matter to me, but it won't matter to him. I understood that from the first." McKenzie got up and walked slowly to his window. I had a horrid feeling he might break down, and I wasn't equipped to handle that. The sense of being suffocatingly enclosed returned: McKenzie's gamble had proved traumatic for everyone. After a few minutes he picked up his manuscript and stuffed it in the envelope, which he sealed and addressed. "If you're so concerned," he said sarcastically, "you'll put this in the mail back home."

"Who's this?"

"An old professor of mine at MIT. He's interested in oceanography and he'll see the manuscript is published anonymously where it will do some good."

"That won't help you, Philip."

"New World either, but other people will use it. And anyway, you forget, I don't exist anymore. Herr Schloder will have other ideas. Who knows what he has in mind, or who he'll meet, or what he'll do. He'll have a different life altogether."

"I thought you'd decided that was just an illusion."

"But it's the illusion of my choice. It'll do for a while. Ah, here's dinner. *Danke*, Hallis."

Dinner came on a cart pushed by a thin dark youth with delicate features and a shy smile. "He's a Turk," McKenzie said briskly when the boy left. "Had kind of a hard life. I think I'll take him with me when I leave. He says he wants to learn English, because he has a cousin or something in Detroit."

"I see."

"I thought you might. There's something you can help me with."

"What's that?"

"Well, Ulrich is taking care of the bills, and I will be starting work in a couple more weeks so money's no problem for me."

"But for Hallis's employment you find yourself a trifle short."

"Yes, and since I'm trusting you with this," he touched the envelope, "I thought you wouldn't miss a couple thousand Deutsche marks in expenses. You can always recoup your losses."

"I suppose so." I gave him some bills.

"I've got to live, you know," he added defensively.

I picked up the envelope and said good-by. I saw a long dismal stretch ahead for Philip.

"Will you mail that or will you hand it in to New World and be the heroine of the moment?"

"I haven't decided yet. It depends on what happens after I get back and what I feel like after the shock wears off. If you give me this, you're going to have to trust my judgment, Philip."

"So long as it doesn't encompass my resurrection. Remember that. I wouldn't want to have to put Dr. McKenzie away literally."

I believed he was serious. "All right. I'll promise you that much."

On the way out, he lingered in the doorway, and I thought perhaps he regretted his decision. "Was it very bad?" he asked. "What happened, I mean."

"Yes, it was. The whole business was very nasty."

"And would it have been worth it, if everything had been on the level?"

"Not to me."

"That's why you'll mail the papers," he said with sudden conviction.

"I haven't promised, Philip."

"I think I can rely on your deviant impulses." We shook hands, and his fingers were cold.

"I won't do anything for a few days, so if you should change your mind — "

"Impossible," McKenzie interrupted. "I must thank Ulrich for a unique opportunity. The dream of my life, although, admittedly not quite in its present form." His voice wavered, and he went on with quick, unconvincing gaiety. "And thank you, too, Anna. I'll see the money's well wasted."

Poor, brilliant, larcenous Philip. As the elevator closed, he was still standing alone at the door of his room. The romantic illusion of liberation had come very dear in his case.

Chapter 19

I WENT STRAIGHT TO THE AIRPORT from the hospital, bought a ticket on the first flight that I could get out of Germany, and called Harry to let him know I was coming home. Early the next afternoon, I unlocked the door of our apartment to find the place empty. Harry had left an apologetic note under a gorgeous vase of roses and isri: he and Jan had been called to a crucial session with the lawyers. Kokpin Novelty, Inc., was almost theirs, and he would be back with the details around five. I put down my suitcase. The house had been closed all day, and it held the warm stuffiness of empty places. I opened the windows, read Harry's note again, nibbled all the petals off a particularly pretty rose, and burst into tears.

This was not one of my usual dietary habits, merely an aberration caused by the events in Trier, but I was still sitting contemplating roses and disasters when Harry opened the door, the bright afternoon sun behind him.

"Hello."

"Hi. How was your meeting?"

"Making progress. What's all this?" he asked, drawing me into his arms.

"Ouch! I cut my forehead."

"Sorry."

I didn't get up but I leaned my head against his side. It was nice to be home. Harry stroked my hair without saying anything for a few minutes.

"Are you all right?"

"No, but nothing too serious."

He patted my arm.

"Ouch!"

"What's that?"

"Tetanus shot."

"I think you'd better give me a quick inventory before I risk kissing you."

My laugh was pretty feeble.

"Heartless woman," he said.

I gave Henry an edited account of the German trip, which he kindly pretended to believe. Two nights later, I woke up with a scream and told him the rest. In my dream, I had been in the amphitheater again, enclosed in its suffocating darkness, and terrified of touching the stone walls I knew surrounded me.

"It's the thing I've always been afraid of most — of being shut in, trapped underground, away from the light. I guess it's going to stay with me for a while."

Harry sat up and leaned against the headboard. "There's more to it than that."

I shrugged.

"You don't have to be a psychiatrist to see what's bothering you."

"Are you going to interpret my dreams or attempt something more scientific?"

There was a pause. Harry began again very quietly and seriously. "You're frightened, because you feel trapped," he said.

"Felt, and was."

"No, present tense. You haven't gone back to your office yet."

"I haven't been well."

"My love, you've got the constitution of a six-day bike racer, and you know it."

"I have a very bad knee. It's a wonder it isn't infected."

"But as a matter of fact it's perfectly fine and your ankle isn't even swollen anymore. What's wrong with you is you're afraid of being trapped in some scheme you can't control."

Silence.

"You've never approved of my job at New World, have you?" That sounded defensive even to me, but Harry refused to be baited.

"I worry about you, you know, but I understood long ago that you needed a certain kind of life, that you needed the stimulus of a certain kind of work. I found that difficult to accept, because I'm just the opposite. I can only take chances in my work when other things are going smoothly. That's why I've been miserable about the damn factory. The kind of muddle you thrive on keeps me from getting anything done."

"I haven't exactly been thriving lately. Maybe I'm getting too old for all this."

Harry shook his head. "You weren't cut out to be a soldier, that's all. There are only two places in an organization where you'll be happy — the very top and the very bottom. You're a crummy subordinate, and you hate to take risks on anyone's orders but your own. That's why you feel trapped, because you know you can't always outsmart the people above you — at least, that's Dr. Radford's diagnosis." He slid down under the covers and yawned. Unlike me, he'd been getting up early in the mornings.

"I suppose I'm afraid of taking the financial risk. Like you — you hesitated long enough before accepting Jan's offer."

"I can't give you advice there, but until you make a decision you can live with, you're not going to feel better."

Harry was right. The horrid suspense and anxiety of the dream lingered into wakefulness and morning, and, more than anything else, it was that nightmarish psychic afterimage which made it impossible for me to return to business as usual. After the scene in the amphitheater, I found that no amount of rationalization could shake my revulsion for the smug self-righteousness that permeated New World. Of course, I realized that there was little one could say to excuse McKenzie, who had cheated his employers and betrayed his colleagues and wasted their work, as well as endangering my life along with his own. There was nothing at all one could say for Jaeger, and probably not much for his brother and their doctor. They were a rotten lot, but they'd been caught up by their greed, while New World's board and officers, equally grasping and quite as cavalier, had remained safe at home. Safety seemed somehow unforgivable, and a disagreeable and rather sad interview with Bertrand Gilson later in the week did nothing to modify my opinion.

I met him in his fancy eyrie above the clouds of D.C. smog. Everything was the same: the large bare desk, the obligatory family photos, the acre or so of subdued plush carpeting — everything but me — I was different. Thanks to greed, incompetence, and Herr Ulrich's curious sense of fair play, I was potentially a very rich and powerful woman. An influential one, too: I had access to the discovery that could put Gilson and me into the petroleum stratosphere — permanently.

We talked about the Jaeger adventure. "Tragic about Dr. McKenzie," Gilson remarked.

I agreed.

"Unstable, of course. You can't run scientists the way you can run management, but there's hell to pay down in the lab."

"Honiss said there were sticky questions being asked."

"Very. McKenzie apparently wasn't keeping his mind on his work."

"Perhaps he'd lost it — I mean his talent for discovery. Maybe that's why he pushed the Jaeger business so hard. To compensate."

"Hmmmm."

I realized I was in an odd position. One word — the truth — and Gilson would open the corporate cornucopia. I smelled the amphitheater and shivered. Gilson was saying there had been some heavy weather over the whole business. He wished like hell Jaeger's papers had been saved and hadn't there been any way?

I listened to him very carefully, but although I could understand every word, their sense eluded me. Gilson might have been speaking a foreign language, and I realized that I'd been wrong about him: our resemblance was only superficial. He was willing to take risks with other people, but he intended to stay safely above the storm himself. That's why he could dismiss McKenzie and Jaeger: they hadn't been important enough to delegate their fears.

"There wasn't, by any chance?"

"Wasn't what, sir?"

"Nothing was left?"

I hesitated only an instant before finding I preferred McKenzie's spontaneous follies to Gilson's more carefully calculated ones. As Philip observed, I have a primitive sense of justice. "No. Jaeger died in the water."

Gilson winced. "There will be problems for you, you realize. The whole affair was turned over to you."

"That is to be expected."

Gilson noticed my tardily suppressed smile. I'm not sure he didn't suspect. We were different, but he had a great sensitivity to deceit; and he must have sensed how great a separation the German business had left between us.

"I don't need to remind you how important success could have been to your career," he said.

"No, I think I see very clearly what it would have meant." I stood up. My days of waiting to be dismissed were over.

Gilson frowned. Then his face closed into a bland, businesslike smile. "Well," he said, "take a few days off. Make sure you're feeling better. Then we'll work up a report for the board."

I had the feeling that he had, with whatever degree of regret, decided to make the best of things — and the best use he could of me. Fortunately I was one jump ahead of him. I went home, got out my typewriter, and shed my corporate skin with two letters: the first, a dignified letter to Gilson, the second, on Harry's ancient, loose-keyed Underwood, an unsigned explanatory note to an elderly professor at MIT. I was just finishing the latter, when the door banged downstairs. Harry was back from the lawyers, and from the sound of his voice there was no doubt they'd gotten the building.

"Anna, Anna, are you home?"

"Yes, I'll be right down."

He came running up the steps two at a time.

"Guess what?"

"You are half-owner of Kokpin Novelty, Inc."

"Wrong. I am half-owner and director of Helios Workshop, which will be open for business in six months."

"Signed, sealed, and delivered?"

"Right! All official. Good-by United Graphics. Good-by lingerie ads and supermarket promotions. We're on our own! Jan's filing the papers in Annapolis right now. We're to pick him up in an hour and start celebrating."

"Congratulations, darling," I said kissing him. "This may call for *several* nights' celebration."

"Well, you and I can see to that. Now get changed and let's go right away. I can't sit still." In honor of his partner, he began dancing a polka around the room.

"All right." I folded the letter to Gilson. Good-by petroleum. "What shall I wear?"

"Something grand."

"Something grand, it is. Oh, let me have one of your business envelopes, would you? A plain one."

McKenzie's manuscript was transferred from a plastic bag in the icebox to the unmarked envelope along with the unsigned explanatory note. Gilson's letter I mailed at the corner. McKenzie's went off to MIT from a mailbox in downtown Annapolis.

"Mysterious missive?" Jan asked.

"Women's organization questionnaire — you know the kind of thing." Jan raised his eyebrows but said nothing.

"Does either of you still have a floor plan with you?"

"I do as a matter of fact," Harry said. "In the car."

"Harry's carried that everywhere for the last month," Jan teased.

"I'd like to see it."

"Right now?"

"Right now."

Harry spread the blueprint over the hood of the car, and I penciled an X through a small office on the second floor. "This one's mine. I'll rent it as soon as you have it in shape."

"Bravo," Jan said, "you're our first tenant. But you're not artistically inclined, and I hope you're not aiming to compete with me."

"No, nothing in the arts at all, but worthwhile. I might even save you money on your insurance."

"For a cut in rent, perhaps?" Jan asked. In business matters, I'm sorry to say, he has the soul of a fish peddler.

"I begin to think you don't want tenants."

"No, no," Harry protested.

"We would be enchanted, of course," Jan said smoothly, "but just what is it you have in mind?"

"A little business of my own. I helped you two with a name for your workshop; now you can give me a hand. Something on the order of Executive Security or some such. Investigative services for companies and executives."

"Discretion guaranteed," Harry said.

"At monstrous cost," Jan added.

"Providing a comfortable profit," I corrected.

"Its sounds," said Harry, "like a much needed addition to an otherwise bohemian firm. That is, I hope so." And he gave me a look. Harry knows more about me than he usually lets on.

"Eminently respectable. In fact I've just guaranteed my integrity."

"I don't see why we shouldn't make a deal," Jan said. "We need to drink to this, Harry."

"Right: to Helios Workshop and What's Its Name."

"To Helios Workshop."

"To What's Its Name."

"You know, I don't like Executive Security," Jan said. "What would you think of — what would you think of Business Protective?"

"Sounds like a truss."

"Or British Insurance."

"Trusty British Insurance?"

"Well — "

"Are you really going to do this?" Harry asked, stopping me.

"Yes."

"About time."

"Yes."

"Are you two coming?" Jan broke in impatiently. "I shall have to do half the drinking and all the dancing myself. Let's see. Private Resources, Sunshine Investigations — that goes with Helios, Corporate Malfeasance, Criminal Intent — how's that, sounds like a crime thriller. We'll hit one yet."

"We'd better celebrate first and pick a name later."

"Hooray! To celebrate," Jan yelled, vaulting into the back seat. Harry gave a war whoop and pulled out into traffic. For someone who had spent the afternoon burning her bridges, I suddenly felt pretty good.